Another Jennifer

by Jane Sorenson

cover illustration by Kay Salem

® STANDARD PUBLISHING

Cincinnati, Ohio   24-03741

Library of Congress Cataloging-in-Publication Data

Sorenson, Jane.
  Another Jennifer.

  (A Jennifer book ; 11)
  Summary: Reminiscing about how they came to be
friends, Jennifer and Heidi discuss what it must feel
like to be a newcomer and to be left out of a group.
  [1. Friendship—Fiction. 2. Prejudices—Fiction.
3. Christian life—Fiction] I. Title. II. Series:
Sorenson, Jane. Jennifer book ; 11.
PZ7.S7214An 1986   [Fic]   86-5788
ISBN 0-87403-088-9

With love to my sister,

Kay Lupi,

who was born when I was Jennifer's age
and who grew up to be my dear friend.

Chapter 1

Our Neighbors' House Is Sold

Lord, it's me, Jennifer.

Don't laugh! I'm sure You don't consider it a big deal, but this was the first morning in my whole life that someone hasn't been there while I've eaten breakfast. Well, not exactly my *whole* life. You know what I mean. Not including vacations or weekends. But never before have I eaten and left for school without having Mom or Grandma there!

Anyhow, because the kitchen light was on, I forgot that today is Mom's first day at computer training. As You know, it is an honor for her to be picked.

While I ate my cereal, I kept hoping my brothers would

come down, if You can believe that one! But Pete and Justin go to school on a later bus. Actually, next year Pete and I'll go together, because then he'll be in junior high too.

Anyhow, I discovered that the cereal on the bottom of the bowl stayed crunchy. That's how much faster I ate because I had nobody except You to talk to.

It was weird not having anybody tell me I looked nice in my pink sweater and not to forget that Dad will be picking me up at the stables this afternoon.

Lord, was Mom lonely this morning? Like, did she wish somebody was there to tell her *she* looked nice? Did she wear the navy suit? The paisley blouse? Did she remember to take boots in case it snowed? I am assuming that she had something to eat before she left!

Personally, I think responsibility is the curse of being the oldest child. Lord, please help me give other people the chance to make their own decisions and mistakes. And please help Mom learn stuff today!

Eating alone is faster.

From the front hall, I could hear my brothers discussing a television program above the sound of hair driers. "Have a good day," I yelled upstairs, but I don't think anybody heard me.

I pulled the front door shut behind me and slowly walked down our lane. The days are getting longer. A few weeks ago, it was still dark when we waited at the bus stop in the morning.

The sign said *sold*. I couldn't believe it. Almost ever

since we moved here, the long ranch house across the road from us has been for sale. All last summer, the lawn service had to pull out the sign so they could mow. In the fall, it was nearly buried with leaves. During the big snow, you couldn't see it at all. Well, to be honest, I didn't really look! But if I had, the sign would have been buried. That's for sure.

No offense, Lord, but I really won't miss the Baldwins. How can you miss somebody you never see? What I have loved is their names! I mean, Dexter Baldwin-the-Second was destined from birth to be a bank president! He probably learned to count using silver dollars.

I looked at Baldwins' house as I walked past. Both times I had seen Mrs. Baldwin, she was wearing a short tennis dress and picking up their black cleaning lady. Mom said her name was Monica. Mrs. Baldwin, that is. Not the black cleaning lady. Mom heard the name from a neighbor. She never met any of them either.

Of course, my friend Chris McKenna's family knows the whole family. That's because they belong to the same clubs and stuff. And, as a matter of fact, the Baldwin kids go to the same private school as Chris. That first summer I was in Philadelphia, I had a fantasy about Dexter Baldwin-the-Third. I figured if I hung around shooting baskets with Justin, Dexter-the-Third would see me and come over. Well, as You know, he didn't. Neither did his sister, Dana, who's exactly my own age. And I've never seen her one time! Ever!

I walked along wondering if I would have liked them.

The Baldwins, I mean. My guess is that I would not. Probably stuck up. Right? Did they avoid our family because we were from Illinois?

"What's on your mind, Jennifer?" Stephanie asked.

Until I get to the bus stop, I never know if she and Lindsay will speak to me or not. "Baldwin's house has a *sold* sign on it," I said.

"I didn't know that," Stephanie said. She sounded surprised. "Daddy didn't mention it."

I decided not to let her get away with it—the one-upmanship game of *my father knows more important people than your father does*. "My daddy didn't either!" I said, grinning.

On the bus, Heidi joined me, like she always does. "Hi, Jennifer! What's new?"

"Not much," I said. "Well, Mom starts computer training today. And the house across the road from us has just been sold."

"Well," Heidi said, "I guess that's more news than we usually have, isn't it? Do you know who your new neighbors will be?"

"Hey, I just saw the sign this morning," I said.

"Maybe they'll have a girl our age."

"Maybe," I agreed. "Or maybe they'll have a boy!"

"Jennifer!" she laughed. "I'm surprised at you!"

"Really?"

"Of course not, silly!" Because Heidi's my best friend, she knows me pretty well. "Is your mom excited about computer training?"

"She is," I said. "But I'm not sure the rest of the family is all that thrilled."

"How come?"

"I guess we're spoiled. Mom's always been there to keep our act together," I said. "It's easy to take that for granted."

"I know what you mean," Heidi agreed.

"Do you think your mother will ever get a job?" I asked.

"I doubt it. She's really into sewing and cooking and gardening and canning and stuff like that," Heidi said.

I nodded. It figured. The whole Stoltzfus family is from Lancaster County. That's where the Amish live.

"Also," Heidi added, "on Tuesday mornings, she bowls."

I just looked at her. "Your mother bowls?"

"Sure. Like I said. On Tuesdays."

I couldn't believe it. "Bowling sure doesn't fit my image of Lancaster County," I said. "I mean, the other stuff I sort of expected."

Heidi laughed. "Don't jump to conclusions, friend!"

"You know," I remembered, "that's what Debby told me. Did I tell you about the missionary's daughter in Haiti? Anyhow, I told her I thought all missionaries were alike. And she thought all the kids in U.S. schools were on drugs!"

Heidi was quiet for a second. "Jennifer, you know what?" she asked.

"No."

"Remember that first time you came to our Sunday school?"

"Uh huh." I remembered like it was yesterday. We had just moved here that week, and I didn't know a soul. That was when Harringtons invited my brothers and me to ride with them to church.

"In the beginning, I didn't think I was going to like you," Heidi said.

I couldn't believe it. Heidi likes everybody. "Why not?" I asked. But I wasn't entirely sure I wanted to hear her answer.

"You looked so cool, Jennifer. I thought you'd think I was some sort of a nerd."

The worst thing is, what Heidi was telling me was true! "Heidi," I told her, "now you're my best friend in the whole world."

"And you're mine, Jennifer!" she said. "Aren't you glad we had time to get past our first impressions?"

Well, we just sat there grinning at each other like ninnies.

"Last stop!" Matthew said, as he headed past us. "Or do you two know something I don't?"

We laughed and followed him off the bus.

Chapter 2

Why Chris Was Smiling

Lord, it's me, Jennifer.

"It's hard for me to concentrate on your riding," Chris said, during a break. "I keep wanting to talk to you."

"To tell you the truth, I'm having the same problem," I admitted. I mean, it's hard when your riding teacher, who is turning into one of your best friends, is sitting there smiling all the time.

Chris winked at me. "Want to hang up the saddle for the afternoon?"

Well, never in a million years did I think I'd ever answer yes to that question! I mean, for me a horse was the maximum fantasy.

But, as You know, I grinned at Chris and headed for the gate. Fortunately, I had taken care of the three stalls first. I clean my own and two others to earn money to sponsor a girl in Haiti. My point is that I was able to groom my horse, Star, right away.

Chris leaned on the stall and watched me. "I keep feeling that I'm going to wake up and find that everything was a dream," she said.

"For instance?" I asked.

"You know. Feeling so happy and accepted. Not feeling so alone anymore. Or so desperate," Chris said. "They say at Alateen that children of alcoholics often hide their feelings."

"Personally, I always thought you were pretty honest," I said.

"With you, maybe. But not with anybody else," she told me. "And I guess I was more honest about my opinions. But not my feelings."

Heavy! But I wanted to see her smile again. "Jason sure likes you!" They had met at a youth group party.

She was right back to smiling. "Do you really think so?"

"You've got to be kidding!" I said.

Chris laughed. "I told you I'm insecure!"

"The truth is, everybody at youth group is excited about you! Chris, did you know that I became a Christian myself at the youth group retreat last fall?"

"Not exactly," Chris said. "But I knew something was different between us. After that, I felt kind of shut out."

12

"I'm sorry," I told her. "It wasn't on purpose."

"I can understand it better now. I mean, wow, now I'd like to talk about God and youth group all the time if I could!"

"Did I do that?" I asked.

"Probably not." She grinned. "You also talked about the Harringtons."

"Well, they were the first guys who ever noticed me," I admitted.

"Like Jason!"

"Right!"

"And you still don't have them sorted out, do you?" she asked.

"What do you mean?" I concentrated on brushing Star.

"You know what I mean! You still haven't decided which one you like best, Matthew or Mack." Good old Chris. Maybe she did hide her feelings. But what she had said was true. She never beat around the bush on other things!

I kept brushing Star. "I'm too young to make a decision," I said. "That's what my grandmother told me."

"It sounds good," Chris replied. "Like a great big cop out! Have your cake and eat it too!"

This wasn't turning out to be as much fun as I thought it was going to be. "If I knew you were going to criticize my relationships, I'd have kept riding," I said.

"Hey, Jennifer!"

"Yes?" I looked up.

"I'm sorry. Really I am! *Live and let live.* That's what I'm learning in Alateen. As you can see, I haven't got it down pat yet."

"I forgive you," I smiled. "How's your mom doing?"

"About the same. But Dad's actually been going to Al-Anon! I really didn't think he'd ever admit we have a problem!" Chris told me.

"Then God's answering your prayer," I reminded her.

"Jennifer, do you pray?"

"Sure," I said. "I tell the Lord everything."

"Doesn't He get tired of hearing it all?" Chris asked.

"He hasn't complained yet," I laughed. "That's one of the greatest things about Him."

"What's another one?" This was Chris McKenna, all right!

"The Lord doesn't only listen," I said. "He has the power to help me."

"That I know!" Chris was smiling again. "I'm suddenly realizing He's doing things for me that I could never do for myself."

"Want a Coke?" I asked. I brought two back from the pop machine, and we sat on a bench. A bench we've sat on many times.

"How's your family?" she asked.

"All right," I said. "Pete's enjoying the drama group and a girl named Madeline Claypool. He and Justin are suddenly buddy-buddy. Mom started computer training this morning. And Dad's worried about something at work."

"And you?"

"I'm feeling terrific! My friend, Chris McKenna, who has taught me all I know about riding, has just become a Christian!" I smiled, and she smiled back.

We just sat there. During the week, Twin Pines is really quiet.

"Say," I told Chris, "this morning I noticed that there's a *sold* sign on Baldwins' house. Did you know they're moving?"

"Sure," Chris said.

"Where are they moving to?"

"They bought land in Chester County and have been building on it for over a year," Chris told me. "Big spread. Even in our circles."

"Chris, did I ever tell you that at first I thought you were poor?"

She laughed so hard she nearly choked. In fact, she couldn't stop laughing. And that got me started. Well, You know what that means!

"I had it figured out that you cleaned stables and gave lessons to pay for your riding," I told her.

"But you still invited me over for dinner?" she asked.

"Sure. We didn't care if you were poor," I told her. "You were nice, and I liked you, and I thought we could be friends."

"That was really super, Jennifer! I'll never forget how much fun I had. Your family seemed like something on television," she said. "So normal, and all those kids!"

"Just three," I said.

"To an only child, it seemed like a dozen," Chris laughed.

"In the beginning, I was worried that you'd be jealous of our house," I giggled. "Then, when I went to yours, I nearly flipped out! It looked like a mansion in a movie or TV! In fact, it still affects me that way!"

"Isn't it funny how people get together?" Chris said.

"Heidi and I were just talking about that this morning on the school bus," I told her. "Just think. If Dad hadn't picked you out as my riding instructor, we'd never have gotten to know each other!"

"Maybe God could have worked out something else," she said.

Rats! I wished I had thought of that first! "Will Dana and Dexter-the-Third still go to your school? I mean, after they move?" I asked.

"Sure," Chris said.

"I wonder who the new people will be?" That was always the first thing we thought of whenever somebody moved in Illinois.

"It would serve you right if they had a fantastic boy your age!" Chris said. "They you'd *really* be mixed up!"

"Heidi and I were thinking maybe they'll have a girl," I said.

Chris grinned at me. "And then maybe both Matthew and Mack will like *her!*"

I groaned. "You've ruined my day!" I teased. Actually, however, it was something to consider!

Just then Felix, the McKennas' chauffeur, stuck his

head in the door. "Ready, Miss Chris?"

She jumped up. "Hey, Jennifer," she said. "Thanks for being my friend!"

"Thanks for being mine!" I told her.

Life really is funny, Lord. Well, not always amusing, but You know what I mean. Are You really in control of who buys which house? And choosing riding teachers? Personally, I think You must be. Otherwise, how would anything ever turn out?

It wasn't even five minutes later that I heard Dad's car horn. I rushed right out, climbed in the front seat, and leaned over to kiss his cheek. Then I fastened my seat belt. "Hi, Daddy!" I said.

He looked at me. "You haven't called me that in a long time! Do you want something?" he laughed.

"I called you that this morning," I told him. "Stephanie was bragging that her daddy hadn't told her Baldwins' house had been sold. Anyhow, I said my daddy hadn't told me either."

"Well, well." He swung onto the highway. "Sounds like a little competition."

"I've always been competitive," I admitted. "I can't help it!"

"We'll let that one go this time," Dad said. "It just happens that I heard today who bought Baldwins' house."

"You didn't!" I said. "Who? Tell me all about them."

"Sorry. I can't do that, because I don't know everything," Dad said. "But I heard at work that our new neighbor will be somebody from EPA."

"What's that?"

"Environmental Protection Agency," my father told me.

"As in forests and air pollution and lakes and nuclear reactors and stuff?"

"Right," Dad said. "And toxic waste."

"So?"

"They're checking into our company," Dad said.

Lord, it sounded like trouble. Possibly bad trouble. At that point, I could either go for it or chicken out. "Wonder how Mom's day went?" I said. "Today was her first day of computer training. Remember?"

Chapter 3

Latest News Update

Lord, it's me, Jennifer.

"Hi, Honey," Dad called when we walked in. "I'm home."

"Hi! I'm in the kitchen." Mom's voice sounded strong and cheerful. Dad hung up his coat and headed back toward the strong and cheerful voice.

I headed upstairs for a quick shower. If I don't change my clothes after horseback riding, nobody wants to sit near me at dinner. In other words, I have no choice.

Pete's door, at the top of the stairs on the left, was, as usual, open. Pete was not, as usual, in there. He used to be home a lot more before he got into drama.

The door on the right was closed. It figured. Mom has

stopped getting on Justin's case for being such a slob. My younger brother spent most of his life in Illinois being grounded. Now, Mom's trying a new approach. Like, anything goes, as long as he keeps his door shut.

"Hi, Jennifer!"

I was nearly in my room at the end of the hall when Justin's door opened. I turned around to see Justin's smile. "I didn't know you were in there," I told him.

"Sometime I'd like to talk to you," he said.

"Great! How about after dinner?"

"I'm on pots and pans."

"Oh, how about if I help you?" I couldn't believe I was saying that. We rotate the three after-dinner kitchen chores. This week I'm on loading.

"I'll just meet you afterwards," he said. "It's personal."

I raised my eyebrows. Well, I think that's what I did. I've never looked in the mirror to find out what happens when I do it. "Your room or mine?" I asked.

"Mine," he said, grinning. He disappeared behind the door.

Actually, I was somewhat curious. Justin and I haven't talked privately for some time. Also, I wondered what his room really looked like! I grinned too.

Not to brag, but my own room is always neat. Is that being responsible? Whatever. Anyhow, messy doesn't blend well with Laura Ashley wallpaper. Also, to be honest, I like being able to find stuff! I stacked my homework on the corner of my desk.

After my shower, I put on clean jeans. Frankly, they are too tight to wear to school. My velour top felt cuddly.

"Hi, Jennifer," Pete said as I passed his room again. He seemed particularly happy.

"Just get home?" I asked. "You look like you had a good day!" Far out! I've got to be more original.

"Far out!" He said. Like he read my mind. It was weird.

"Well?" I waited.

"Now that I've stopped trying so hard to get the kids to like me, they do. Like me, that is!"

"I'm glad," I told him. Frankly, I'm not sure if it was more painful for him or the rest of the family while he was trying to find himself. Well, he wasn't exactly lost, but You remember, I'm sure. "Going downstairs?"

He joined me. "Respect!" Pete said. "I got respect."

"You *have* respect," I muttered.

"Right! I do!"

"So, what happened today?" By now we were in the foyer.

"Well, we chose teams for a special social-studies project. And I was the first one picked!"

"You've always been good at social studies," I reminded him.

"That never helped before! But I've got it figured out. It's Madeline Claypool."

"Huh?"

"Well, Madeline Claypool's the prettiest girl in our room!" he said.

"She chose you?" I asked.

"Of course not. She's on Jeff's team," he said.

"I don't get it," I said. "And we're going to miss dinner if you don't get to the point."

"OK," he said. "I'll take it from the top. See, when I joined the drama group, Madeline Claypool started noticing me. So I started liking her. I mean, I really liked her before, but there was no point. The prettiest girl in the class isn't going to like the class wimp!" he explained. "But now that Madeline Claypool likes me, suddenly I got respect."

"You *have* respect," I muttered.

"Right!" he said. "You've finally got it."

I wasn't exactly sure. "Is Madeline nice?" I asked.

"Madeline Claypool is beautiful!" Pete said.

I was getting sick of her, and we hadn't even met! "And how's it with Walter?" I really hated to bring it up. He's the fat one the guys called "Hippo."

"He's on the same team I am," Pete said. "Picked last."

It figured. "Maybe you could help him," I said.

"Not yet," Pete told me. "I just got respect myself."

Well, Lord, I suppose You noticed at dinner that at least most of us are happy. Our table conversation defies description. That means we talk a lot.

"I have a streak going," Justin reported. See, Lord, when you tell the family something, it isn't considered bragging. It's called communicating.

"Cruddiest room?" Mom suggested.

22

"You said the room is up to me," Justin grinned. "My news is that I've made my last four free throws."

"What's the record?" Dad wondered.

"I don't know. It was set before we moved here. But I'm going for the longest record in modern times," Jus explained.

"The neat thing about sports is that being good is easy to measure," Pete said.

"I agree," I said. "Nobody keeps records on kindness, or sharing, or stuff like that." Suddenly, I realized what I was saying. "Well," I added, "Of course, the Lord does!"

"Sue, tell us about your day." Dad never calls her "Mom" like the rest of us do. Naturally. That isn't her name.

"Pretty basic so far," she said. "I wonder if it's necessary to learn the history of computers in order to operate one?"

"Are you the oldest person?" Pete asked.

"About half are reentry women."

"Astronauts?" Justin was amazed.

Mom smiled. "Reentry people are people who've been out of the job market while their children were young."

"Any men?" I asked.

"Several," Mom reported. "But none as nice as your father."

Suddenly, I realized what was different. Dad's usually the one who carries the ball at dinner. We've always depended on him to put the sparkle in our mealtimes. And tonight, he was just sitting there.

"Something wrong, Dad?" Pete had noticed too.

"I'm really tired," Dad said.

"Do you have to go back to the office?" Mom asked.

"I'm afraid I do. I'd rather stay home. You know that, I hope."

"Of course, Peter," Mom said. "Try not to be too late."

"I see the house across the road is sold," Justin said. "Anybody know anything about the new people?"

"He works at EPA," Dad said. "Environmental Protection Agency."

"Oh, I forgot to tell you." Pete was so excited, he practically interrupted. "Their name is 'King' and they have two kids. Justin, you're finally going to have a boy your age in the neighborhood!"

"All right!" Justin cheered.

"What about the other kid?" I asked

"Guess what?" Pete reported. "A girl named Jennifer!"

I couldn't believe it! "How old?"

"Eighth grade," Pete answered. I nearly fainted.

"How did you find out all that?" Dad asked.

"Scott told me. You know, Scott Franklin. Lives down past Harringtons. His mom's gone into real estate."

"When are they moving in?" Mom asked.

"If Scott's right, real soon." Pete had a strange look on his face.

"Is something wrong?" Dad asked.

"Jeff said his father will blow his top when he hears about it!" Pete said.

We all sat there waiting. Finally Justin asked. "Well, why?"

"The King family is black," Pete said.

We all just sat there. I mean, nobody said anything. As You know, we've never had a black family live in our neighborhood before. We have no experience.

"I'm sure they'll be lovely," Mom said.

"How can you tell?" I asked. "I mean, you haven't even met them."

"I'll take over some cookies," Mom said. "Chocolate chip."

"Do you have time? You're gone all day," I reminded her.

"Well, gang, I've got to get back to work." Dad pushed his chair back from the table.

I really expected our father to give us his pep talk about prejudice. How this speedy guard on his team in high school was black, etc. But this time Dad didn't. So there was this awkward pause. That's what they call it in stories. That means nobody said anything at all.

"Who's on loading?" Mom asked, finally.

So I started filing the plates into the dishwasher. When I finished, Justin was still standing at the sink. Naturally. That's what pots and pans is all about. "See you later," I told him. "Let me know when you're done." He nodded.

I had just finished organizing my homework when he knocked at my door. "Come on in, Jus," I said.

He walked in and looked around. "Maybe we should just talk in here," he said.

"Whatever." I turned around my desk chair and Justin sat in the bean bag.

My brother was smiling. "Ever since we moved here, I've been praying for a guy my age in the neighborhood," Justin said. "I'll bet he's a star at sports. We can come home from practice together."

"Did you already know about Kings?" I asked. "Before dinner?"

"Nope. I hadn't seen Pete since I got home," he said.

"So that's not what you really wanted to talk about?"

"No." He started grinning again.

"Not another girl friend!" I guessed.

"She isn't anything at all like Nicole," Justin told me. "She's kinda shy."

I waited.

"She's awfully smart in math."

"Pretty?" I asked.

"Not exactly," my brother said. "But somehow it doesn't seem to matter."

"Sounds serious." I smiled at him.

"Do you think it's too soon after Nicole for me to handle another meaningful relationship?" Justin asked.

I didn't want to laugh. I mean, he's only in fourth grade, mind You! "Is that what's bothering you, Justin?"

"Sort of," he said. "I mean, I like her a lot, except for one thing." He paused. "She has crooked teeth. Sort of like a witch."

"Before long, she'll be in braces," I said. "Along with most of the class." It seems like I've had mine on forever! "That's it?"

"Don't laugh," Justin said. "But she doesn't even know I exist!"

This time I really couldn't help it. I laughed so hard that it was catching, and Justin started laughing too. He had no choice. I'll bet we laughed for five minutes.

It wasn't until after he left that I realized Justin never did tell me the girl's name. Is she someone who knows You, Lord?

Chapter 4

There Goes the Neighborhood

Lord, it's me, Jennifer.

Breakfast today wasn't as bad as yesterday. For one thing, Mom had left me a "happy face" note saying she loves me. Two more were addressed to Pete and Justin. I hope Dad got one too!

But, although I felt happier, I still ate just as fast. Which meant I got to the bus stop early. In fact, except for two seventh-grade guys, I was the very first one there.

"Well, well," said Matthew. "Good morning, Jennifer!" He and Mack walked toward me. At first, Mack just grinned. I've observed that when they're together, Matthew does most of the talking.

"Hi!" I said. Brilliant, Jennifer! Really cool!

"How's Chris?" Mack asked. "Did you see her yesterday afternoon?"

"She's doing great!" I said. "She told me she's never felt so happy and accepted."

"Our youth group is pretty special that way," Matthew said. "Some groups aren't friendly to new people. And I've even heard of one that's full of cliques."

"Not to mention kids who make it tough for anyone who's different," Mack added.

"You know," I said, "you just made me remember something. Last fall, when I went on that retreat, I noticed how well Andy was accepted. It really impressed me."

"Well, that's the way it's supposed to be for Christians," Matthew said. "Jesus loves everybody. We know that in our heads, but we don't always act it out."

"If I had been treated like an outsider, I probably wouldn't have wanted to come back," I said.

"I just got an idea," Matthew said. "What if we asked Chris and Jason to go to the high-school basketball game with the four of us? We could go to Reuben's afterwards, like we usually do. Do you think Chris would like that?

"I think she would," I said. "Want me to ask her?"

"Sure," Matthew said. "Why don't you check with Heidi about it too, and I'll see Jason at lunch."

"What if Chris can't come?" I asked.

"Should we wait and see?" Mack wondered.

"Sounds good, Mack," his brother said. "For now, Jennifer, why don't you ask Heidi and Chris? And let us know, OK?"

29

"Fine," I said.

I glanced at my watch. The bus was going to be late again. By now, the rest of the kids had assembled on the corner. The other guys formed a cluster. And, as usual, Stephanie Cantrell and Lindsay Porterfield stood together.

Stephanie has one of those voices that isn't really loud, but it sort of stands out. You know what I mean.

"Daddy says it's going to be a disaster!" she was saying. "All the property values in the neighborhood will go down. He says we won't be able to give away our houses!"

"What's Stephanie upset about now?" Matthew wondered.

I wanted to chicken out and not get involved. I shrugged my shoulders. But it didn't work. Lord, I'm so honest, I can't even tell a lie silently!

"I'm not sure it's true," I said, "but Pete heard that the family buying Baldwins' house is black."

"So?" Mack asked.

Stephanie kept talking. "Daddy says they never keep up their property. Just look at the housing developments in the city—filthy, graffiti on all the walls, high crime rate!" She paused and took a breath.

"But this isn't the city, Stephanie," Lindsay said. Believe it or not, I could have hugged her!

"Of course not," Stephanie replied. "That's Daddy's point, exactly. This is Main Line Philadelphia."

"But wouldn't they have to have lots of money to buy

that big house? Nothing around here is cheap," Lindsay said.

By now, all the kids on the corner were listening in.

"What my father wants to know is why Baldwins would even sell to them," Stephanie said. "And, if I know Daddy, he'll find out!"

I felt very uncomfortable. "Do you think we should say something?" I asked.

Mack looked at Matthew. Matthew kind of narrowed his eyes. He does that sometimes when he's thinking.

Well, just at that point the bus came around the corner. So whatever Matthew decided didn't matter anyway. We all climbed on. The Harringtons went on back to sit with their boy friends, and I waited for Heidi. I felt rotten.

"Hi, Jennifer!" Heidi said. "Are you OK?"

"Sure," I said, making myself smile. "The bus sure was late, wasn't it?"

"Right," she said. "I'm glad it isn't too cold."

"I had a nice chat with Harringtons," I told her.

"Oh?"

"They want us to go with them Saturday to the high-school game," I said. "And I'm supposed to see if Chris can join us. If she can go, Matthew's going to ask Jason."

"No dates?" Heidi asked.

"They didn't exactly say so," I replied. "But it sounds more like a group thing."

"Will it work?" Heidi wondered.

"We'll see," I said. My mind wasn't totally on the weekend plans. I sat there a minute trying to decide

31

whether or not I should tell her about the Kings.

"Have you found out anything about the new neighbors?" Heidi asked.

"Only what Peter heard at school," I said.

"Well?"

I didn't know where to start. "Mr. King works for EPA. That's Environ. . . ."

"I know what it is," Heidi said. "Go on."

"Well, they have two kids exactly like your family and mine," I said. "A boy Justin's and Keever's age. And a girl our age."

"Great!" Heidi asked. "I don't think we could handle another guy anyhow." She laughed.

"Her name's Jennifer," I said.

"No kidding! We'll have to figure out a way to tell you two apart."

"I don't think it will be hard," I told her.

"How do you know?" Heidi giggled.

"The Kings are black," I said.

"Oh," she said. "Sorry. I didn't mean to be crude. I had no idea."

"It's OK," I said. I looked back at Stephanie and Lindsay. "If you want crude, she's sitting behind us."

"Lindsay?" Heidi guessed.

I shook my head. "Stephanie quoted her 'daddy' at the bus stop. He sounds like a real bigot," I said.

"What's that?"

"You know, prejudiced. No understanding of what democracy is all about."

32

"Lots of people used to be that way," Heidi said.

"Maybe some people still are," I told her.

"How sad! Then we'll just have to be extra nice to make up for the bigots." She smiled. "Won't we?"

"Right," I said. I decided not to mention my father's company and toxic waste. Enough is enough! Already the morning had dumped a heavy load on my shoulders. Lord, please lift the weight!

"What shall we wear Saturday night?" Heidi asked.

I smiled. "Skirts?"

"Excellent!" she said. "I sure hope Chris can come!"

*   *   *   *   *   *   *   *

Well, Stephanie kept her big mouth shut during lunch. Which was just as well, because I probably would have let her have it. And I'm not sure that's Your plan. Is it?

And after school, out at Twin Pines, Chris was on cloud nine. It seems that Jason had already called her last night to invite her to the basketball game.

"It's my first date," she said. "I can't believe it!"

"Well," I said, "then maybe you'd rather not come with the rest of us."

"Are you kidding? I've never gone to a game with a group of kids in my whole life!" She practically danced up and down.

"Then I'll have Harringtons call Jason," I said. "They'll have to work out the driving and stuff."

"Oh, we're all set," Chris told me. "That is, if you all don't mind riding with Felix."

"You told Jason about Felix?" I said.

"I had to. He was picking me up after the youth group Valentine Party, remember?"

I giggled. "And what did Jason say?" I mean, in our group, having a real live chauffeur isn't exactly par for the course!

Chris giggled too. "He said the whole thing sounded pretty handy to him, and he wouldn't hold it against me!"

"Good for old Jason!" I cheered. "And, just think. This weekend, for once, Mr. Harrington won't have to be invisible!"

"Huh?"

I explained to Chris how we always needed a father to drive, since Matthew won't get his license until next year. And how good Mr. Harrington had gotten at ignoring us and being ignored. When he was the driver, he was practically invisible!

"That's really funny," Chris laughed. "I hope Felix does as well!"

Anyhow, I was back to feeling marvelous. We both cleaned our stalls, and then we both rode our horses. And, by the time we had finished grooming Star and Hoagie, I had forgotten all about the King family.

Chapter 5

In the
Main Stream

Lord, it's me, Jennifer.

Not much to report. It seems like Dad is working more and liking it less. While Mom is blooming, he is fading. Please help my father!

Until today, nothing special has been happening at school. Unless You call getting more and more homework special. Personally, I do not. I've always liked school, mainly because I'm good at it. But recently I've found myself waiting for afternoons and the weekend.

Stephanie quit talking about the King family, which is quite a relief. Now she and Lindsay are back to ignoring me.

As for Heidi, her announcement on the bus this morning brought the biggest surprise in several days. "I've got a job!" she told me, as soon as she sat down.

"No kidding!" I said. "Doing what?"

"Helping the woman who lives across the street," Heidi said. "Mrs. Floyd's been trying to find somebody to clean her house. Mom just heard about it yesterday. I went over, and she hired me!"

"You mean like dusting and vacuuming?" I asked.

"Sure. And ironing, And cleaning bathrooms. The whole bit. Whatever needs doing," she said.

"Like toilets?" I asked. Softly, of course.

"Naturally," Heidi said. "Jennifer, don't you ever clean toilets?"

"Not when I can get out of it," I admitted. "And it sounds even more yucky doing it for strangers. If you really want to work, can't you find something else?"

"Jennifer, Mrs. Floyd has twins, and she needs me! Besides, I'm too young to get a regular job. And I'm really good at cleaning. My mom has been training me all my life."

"How often?" I asked. "I mean at Mrs. Floyd's."

"For now, three times a week," she said. "I thought you'd be glad for me, Jennifer."

"It seems so degrading," I admitted.

"Worse than cleaning stables?" she laughed.

I laughed too. "No, I guess not. It just doesn't seem very professional. How will it look on your resume?"

"Who cares?" Heidi said. "I suppose washing people's

feet wouldn't look good either. But Jesus did it!"

"You win," I said. "It's funny, Heidi. It isn't hard for me to picture myself as a servant to the people in Haiti. But not around here."

"Jennifer." Heidi smiled at me. "I just love your honesty!"

I shrugged my shoulders. "Maybe I'll change," I said.

"Please don't," she said. "I mean about being honest. There's so little of it around anymore. So many fakes."

When the bus stopped, we split up and headed for our lockers. Fate had put mine next to Mack Harrington's. Well, actually, they had been assigned alphabetically! This morning, Mack was waiting for me.

I smiled at him. "Hi," I said.

"Hi, yourself!" Mack smiled too. "Can I walk you to homeroom?"

"Sure," I said. "Just let me get my act together." I hung up my coat, and got out the books and homework I'd need for my morning classes.

"Jennifer, it seems like I never get to talk to you anymore," he said. "You sit there in front of me every day, and we might as well be strangers."

"I take it you aren't planning to risk more detentions," I said. Lord, You probably remember the last time he talked to me in class. The time Mr. Hoppert gave him an eight o'clock detention and his parents made him walk to school.

"This is probably a better way," he grinned.

Since our bus had been on time, we didn't have to

hurry. We walked along slowly. Frankly, I didn't notice even one other person in the hall. Which is ridiculous. "Chris is really excited about going to the game," I said.

"So is Jason!" Mack told me. "He's fallen for Chris like a ton of bricks!"

I laughed. "My grandfather used to say that," I said. "I mean about the ton of bricks."

"So did mine!" He laughed too. "Jennifer, I didn't realize Chris's family was rich," he said. "You never mentioned it."

"No offense," I said. "But there are lots of things I don't tell everybody, Mack. Chris was really my first friend in Pennsylvania. And nothing else mattered."

"Hey, lighten up!" Mack grinned. "You're a terrific friend, Jenny. That's just one of the things I like about you."

He hardly ever calls me "Jenny." Most people don't. "I want to keep being your friend, Mack," I told him.

"And Matthew's too?" he asked.

"Yes," I said. "If that's possible."

Mack really didn't answer, but he smiled. We had stopped in front of our homeroom. "Just remember, Friend, I'm always behind you!" He laughed. It was kind of a joke since he sits right behind me, so I laughed too. Then we went in.

When the bell rang, everybody settled right down. Mr. Hoppert is a no-nonsense kind of teacher. Frankly, I admire that. He gave the usual announcements about not throwing food in the lunchroom, and next week's tryouts

38

for a new play, and the school band is low on trumpets.

"I've also been asked to read the following announcement from the principal," Mr. Hopper said. We waited. *"'The Special Education Department is announcing a new program of integrating students for certain classes when this seems appropriate. This will comply with the directives of the Commonwealth of Pennsylvania. We expect complete cooperation of our faculty and students in this effort.'* Are there any questions?" Mr. Hoppert asked.

"Yeah," Scott said. "What does it mean?"

Everybody laughed. Except Mr. Hoppert. He was serious. Even more serious than when he talks about improper agreement of subjects and pronouns. "Have you heard of *mainstreaming?"* he asked.

Nobody answered. Personally, I thought it sounded like something to do with drugs, but I wasn't sure. And, naturally, I didn't want to make a fool out of myself.

"You are probably aware that schools are now required by law to provide an education for students who are impaired—mentally, physically, and emotionally," Mr. Hoppert explained. "This was not always the case. Not too many years ago, handicapped children were just kept at home or sent to special schools."

Stephanie raised her hand. "You mean the retards and cripples and crazies?" She was showing off. I could tell.

I sucked in a breath. As You know, I hated what Stephanie had said and I felt embarrassed for her. Mostly I was disgusted with her.

"That's exactly who I mean!" Mr. Hoppert said. "However, I find your choice of terms to be crude and distasteful. You will never use those words again in this room!"

As Grandma says, you could have heard a pin drop.

"In recent years, our country has been taking another step in its care of the handicapped," Mr. Hoppert continued. "Whenever possible, local communities have been encouraged to care for these people."

I tried to listen carefully. To be honest, I haven't known any handicapped people. Not even in Illinois.

"*Mainstreaming* is the term used to describe including handicapped students in regular classrooms," Mr. Hoppert explained. "Although disadvantaged children need the support of special teachers and programs, many think they can benefit by attending certain classes with so-called 'normal' students."

It sure sounded like we might be getting some handicapped kids in our classes. Whether Stephanie liked it or not. And maybe she wasn't the only one!

Mr. Hoppert smiled. "I know I can count on you," he said. "My own opinion is that the rest of us have a lot to learn from the so-called *special* people! Any questions?"

"I really feel like I want to help, but I'm scared," I admitted. "What if we blow it?"

"I'm not sure I have all the answers," Mr. Hoppert said. "But maybe there are some things we can work on together to better prepare us. Let me work on it!" He smiled again.

40

I relaxed. It was good to have somebody like Mr. Hoppert in charge! Please help him, Lord!

In the afternoon, after my riding lesson, I asked Chris if she had ever heard of *mainstreaming*.

"Handicapped kids, right?" she said.

"Uh huh. Do you have them in your school?"

"Not exactly." She laughed. "Mine is the kind of school parents enroll their kids in when they're born to make sure they get in," she said.

"Normal rich kids," I said.

"If you want to put it that way," she replied. "But did you know there's a special school near here for emotionally handicapped kids? It's supposed to be one of the best in the country," Chris told me. "And it isn't exactly cheap either! Also, there's an excellent home for retarded kids."

"Chris, remember last summer?" I asked her. "Before I really knew you? Well, anyhow, Mom heard about that school, and we thought that's where you went!"

Chris laughed. "You've got to be kidding! Why would you think that?"

"Well, you were so mysterious about your family. And you said you went to a private school. Mom and I just put two and two together," I said.

Chris laughed again. "Speaking of handicapped kids, did you know that horseback riding is excellent therapy for them? I read that in one of my riding magazines."

"I never heard that," I said.

"Would you be interested in helping someone learn?" Chris asked.

"Me?" I said. "I'm still learning myself!"

"You don't have to be on the Olympic team to teach a handicapped kid," Chris said.

"How come you haven't done it?"

"I just never considered it," she replied. "Partly because I've been coaching you," she said. "You retard!"

"Don't say that, Chris! I don't think it's funny!"

"Sorry," Chris said. "I don't either. Not really."

"Personally, I'm kind of chicken. But do you think we could work together to help a handicapped kid?" I asked. "It would be a super way to show love for somebody who needs it."

"I need love myself," Chris said. "Have you forgotten?"

"Of course not," I said.

Chris gets right to the point. "You're right, it is scary. Are you disappointed in me?" she asked.

"No, I'm not," I said. "But it's something for us to think about."

I remembered her rough life at home. And I remembered to be thankful that my mom isn't an alcoholic. "Hey, Chris." I smiled at her and winked. "Mack told me that Jason's fallen for you like a ton of bricks!"

"It sounds like terrific news!" She grinned. "But what do bricks have to do with it?"

"Forget it!" I laughed. "An expression like that is no good if you have to explain it!"

"But Jason does like me?"

"To the max," I said smiling. "Like he thinks you're the greatest!" This time she caught on!

Chapter 6

The Family Meets Walter

Lord, it's me, Jennifer.

I hadn't realized Walter was coming over. He was there when Mom and I got home. See, Dad was out of town, so she had to pick me up after she got home from her computer training. Well, anyhow, we walked in through the den and into the family room, and there he was.

"Walter, this is my mom and my sister, Jennifer," Pete said.

"Hi," I said. I shook his outstretched hand.

"Hi, Jennifer," he said. He didn't smile, but his eyes seemed kind.

"Hello, Walter." Mom smiled. "I didn't catch your last name."

"Sorry," Pete said. He was embarrassed.

"Giordano," said Walter. Then he offered his hand toward Mom. "Hi, Mrs. Green." He was smiling now.

"Well," Mom said, "I'd better get something going in the kitchen."

"And I need a shower." I grinned. "I'm afraid I smell pretty horsy!"

"See you later," Pete said. He gave me a special smile.

"Can we help you, Mrs. Green?" Walter asked. I think Mom nearly fainted.

I headed upstairs. Frankly, Lord, I was pretty surprised myself. When Pete first told me Walter had a weight problem, I had pictured a short, fat nerd. Naturally, cruel kids would call him "Hippo" behind his back! Not that doing it was kind or OK. But that's life.

I never really put it into words, but, to be honest, I guess I thought Walter's story had three possible endings. Maybe somebody like Pete could help him see that You love him no matter what size he was. Or he'd diet and work out, and his life would get better. Or else, Walter would learn to take the name calling with humor, and get on with it. Otherwise, he'd be in for a life of misery.

Well, maybe I was wrong. For starters, Walter sure doesn't look like I thought he would. Not at all! He's not short and fat and flabby and spineless. He's taller than Mom! Considering his height, he's probably not overweight at all. I mean, this is one large dude!

By the time I showered and got dressed, Pete and Walter were laughing in the kitchen.

"I'm an expert on salads," Walter told Mom, as he

pulled lettuce apart. "Do you happen to have a few hard-boiled eggs and some croutons?"

"Can I help too?" I asked.

"Just the napkins," Mom told me. "The boys have taken care of everything else."

"Where's Justin?" I asked.

"He went to the library," Mom said. "Mrs. Stoltzfus is bringing him home." She glanced at the clock.

As he tossed the salad in a large bowl, Walter looked like a chef. "I hear Justin's very athletic," he said. "Pete's very proud of him."

"Well, he's good," Pete said. "Even though he is my brother!"

"You're really lucky, Pete," Walter said. "To have a brother and sister."

"You're an only child?" Mom asked.

"That's right," Walter said. "I live with my mom. I never knew my father. He died before I was born. But Mom's the greatest!"

"Sometime you'll have to meet Dad," Pete said. "I'd be proud to share him with you!"

Walter looked up from the salad and smiled. "Thanks," he said. "I'd really like that."

There was a draft through the kitchen, followed by Justin's yell, "I'm home!"

"We're in the kitchen," Mom said. "Close the door, please."

"I did," Justin said, as he joined us. He took one look at the giant tossing our salad and let out a whistle.

45

"Wow!" he said. "I feel like Jack and the Beanstalk!"

Everybody laughed. Even Walter. "Which are you, Jack or the beanstalk?" he asked, looking down at our small brother.

"Maybe I have the wrong story!" Justin laughed. "The truth is, you look more like a lineman for the Eagles!"

"I'm not into sports," Walter said. No apology. Just stating a fact.

"Rotten luck!" Justin said. "I think they could use you!"

"Jus, this is my friend, Walter Giordano," Pete said. "Walter, my brother Justin."

When Walter smiled, his eyes crinkled up at the corners. He reminded me of a teddy bear. He put down the salad tongs and gave Justin his paw. "I'm honored," he said. And it wasn't a put-down. You could just tell.

"Same here," said Justin.

"Lasagna's ready!" Mom announced. "You can all take your places, and I'll bring it in."

We sat in the kitchen. Walter took Dad's chair. Naturally. It was the only one empty. Frankly, he looked right at home!

"Jennifer," Mom said, "do you want to pray?"

Ignoring Walter and everybody else, I bowed my head and closed my eyes. "Thanks, Lord for our family. Bless Dad, wherever he is. Thank You that Walter can be with us. And thanks for this good meal. Bless us as we enjoy it. Amen."

Dinner turned out to be a mellow time. Mom had put

candles on the table, and for once, nobody made any smart-aleck remarks.

"Where's Dad?" Justin asked.

"Boston," Mom said.

"Are you and Pete working on your social-studies project?" I asked Walter.

"Not tonight," he said. "Of course, our group is starting to work on it."

"What's your subject?" Mom asked.

"The group decided to do it on Haiti," Walter said. "Actually, it was Pete's idea."

"That figures." I smiled. "Let me know if I can help." Ever since I went to Haiti with Grandma, everyone in the family has been doing projects on the tiny country. The Greens probably know more about Haiti than any family in the United States!

"Walter, how come you don't play football?" Justin asked. "No offense, but at your size, you're a natural."

"Good one!" Pete approved. "When you said, 'no offense,' I mean."

The guys all laughed. "I guess *I'm* just a natural!" Justin replied. Mom and I laughed too. I didn't get it, but I didn't want to just sit there, so I faked it.

"Well," Walter said, "the truth is I don't care for the violence. See, Justin, I was always bigger than other kids. As far back as I can remember, I wanted to be friends with them, but because I was so much bigger, I often knocked them down. Kids were always afraid of me, because they thought I might hurt them."

47

"Maybe when the weather gets better, we could just pass a football around," Justin said. "Our dad used to play."

"Maybe Walter isn't interested," Mom said. "Not everyone is."

"Right," Pete laughed. He should know! Mr. Uncoordinated, in person!

"Sometimes I watch the pro games on TV," Walter said. "But, I really don't have time for sports."

I was very surprised. Here I was picturing a guy who needed something to do to fill up his empty hours. And he was saying he didn't have time. Well, of course! Naturally, lots of kids who aren't athletic use that for an excuse. That must be it!

"Then what *are* you into?" Justin asked.

I could have killed him. Justin, that is. Get off Walter's case! I tried to think of a way to change the subject. Quick.

But before I could say a word, Walter was standing up next to the table. He waved his napkin and smiled. "Walter's my name. And magic's my game!" He reached over and took a hard-boiled egg from behind Mom's ear. With a flourish, he handed it to her.

Sorry about the pun, Lord, but we all cracked up!

Finally, things got quiet and Walter sat down. "How'd you do that?" Pete asked. Walter just laughed.

"Hey, you're all right!" Justin gave his approval. "Do you ever give performances?"

Walter laughed. "Well, my mom's a good audience,"

48

he said. "And in a few weeks, I'm doing a show for my Boy Scout troop."

I couldn't believe it. As You know, when I think of Boy Scouts, I naturally think of little kids. It wasn't all that long ago that Matthew Harrington and I laughed our heads off at the thought of *his* being a Boy Scout. I looked back at Walter again. He was serious.

Well, I guess nobody else knew quite what to say either. We all just sat there.

Walter wasn't embarrassed at all. He smiled his gentle, teddy bear smile. I felt just like hugging him! Which was pretty embarrassing. For me, that is. Naturally, Walter didn't know!

"You seem surprised," he said. "I don't usually tell people I'm in Scouts, because I think they'd tease me. And I already get as much of that as I can take." He looked at Pete. "In fact, once in a while, too much."

"You're great, Walter," Pete said. And I could tell he meant it.

"I guess I have no choice now but to trust you," Walter said. "The cat's out of the bag! Anyhow, I'm in a Boy Scout troop over in Phoenixville. I'm working on my Eagle rank. But, mostly I try to help with the younger guys. Lots of them don't have fathers either, so I understand how they feel."

Suddenly, I could feel my eyes filling up with tears. I blinked hard and looked away. The last thing in the world I wanted to do was cry.

"You're a very special person, Walter," Mom said.

"Thank you, Mrs. Green." He smiled. "Mom thinks so too, but I'm sure she's prejudiced."

Well, we had finished eating, and there wasn't any dessert. I remembered that Pete's job this week is clearing the table. "Pete, I'll clear," I told him. "You guys helped Mom before."

"Thanks, Jennifer," my brother said. "Want to play a little Ping-Pong, Walter?" They headed for the basement.

"I'll help clear too, Jennifer," Justin said.

"Only if you let me help with pots and pans," I told him.

"It's a deal!" Justin grinned from ear to ear.

While we worked, he told me he had made two more free throws. He didn't mention the girl at all, and I didn't ask.

*   *   *   *   *   *   *

Well, as You know, I didn't see Walter again. Back in my room, I sat down at my desk and just looked at the closed books. I pictured those guys from school taunting Walter in the sweater department at the mall. Calling him "Hippo" over and over. Embarrassing him in public until he broke down and cried.

Now, knowing Walter, I felt the pain even more intensely than I had when Pete first described the scene to me.

This time I couldn't stop my tears. I didn't even try.

Chapter 7

A Strong Dose
of the Past

Lord, it's me, Jennifer.

This morning I woke up thinking about (surprise!) Walter! Although I had never seen him before last night, I feel like I have known someone like him before. But where? Figuring out the answer to that is kind of like trying to find something you've lost. You look in all the obvious places first.

While I was getting dressed, my mind flew back to Illinois. Was it Bernard Hotchkiss, who carried a briefcase in kindergarten? Not really. Arthur Murray? Nope. Was it Freddy the Funk in fourth grade? No way.

By the time I sat down to eat my cereal, I still hadn't figured it out. Although I've known my share of "picked on" kids, Walter wasn't like any of them.

Eating alone is more fun if you have something to think about. Lord, does Walter remind You of someone?

The puzzle was still unsolved when I headed out the front door. Across the road, three small moving trucks were parked.

I gasped. It was just like seeing the man with white hair in church. See, right after my grandpa died, every time I saw a man with white hair, for just a second I'd think it was Pops! It was like I had a computer in my head, programmed to go off. My mind knew Grandpa Green was gone, but the old feelings kept coming back. At the most unexpected times. Like when I saw white hair.

Did You wonder if I had a point? Well, when I saw those trucks, a lot of old tapes in my mind started to go off. I mean, I've hardly thought about moving in months! But, suddenly, the feelings returned. I started feeling excited. And sad. And afraid. That's how I felt when I knew we were moving here.

I read the name on the trucks. Of course! Baldwins are using the same moving company we did. The small trucks are used by the packers. It was all coming back to me.

Moving was my biggest adventure before Haiti. To tell the truth, those are the only real adventures I've ever had. Frankly, I can't believe we moved just last year! My whole life has changed. *I've* changed. Everybody in my family has changed!

Well, I had to get on with it, or I'd miss the school bus.

"Hi, Jennifer!" Mack said. He and Matthew were standing together smiling.

52

"We'll pick you up at 7:30 tomorrow night. OK?" Matthew asked.

"Great!" I said. There's nothing like a strong dose of the present to wipe away those old computer tape memories!

"Did you know we're riding with Chris McKenna's chauffeur?" Matthew asked.

"His name is Felix," I said. "He's married to Nellie. And he's a great guy."

"I'm glad," Matthew said. "And here I thought it was just a way of getting somewhere without our parents," he laughed.

I felt kind of put down. Which probably was stupid. After all, just because I've gotten to know Felix doesn't mean other people won't be blown away by riding with a chauffeur. Still, Felix is a special person!

"Something wrong, Jennifer?" Mack asked.

"I'm OK." I made myself smile.

* * * * * * * *

Heidi was breathless when she climbed on the bus. "I had to run," she said, as she collapsed next to me.

"You never have to run," I observed. "What happened?"

She grinned. "You'll never believe this. I was daydreaming!"

"OK." I grinned back. "What happened?"

"How did you know something happened?" Heidi asked.

"You dope! I can read your mind!" I laughed.

"Well, since you already know, I won't have to tell you!"

"Details?" I asked. "You know I can't fill in the details."

Heidi blushed. "Well," she said. "It's not that big a deal."

"Hurry up!" I said. "You're making me crazy."

She blushed again. "Last night Matthew Harrington called."

"So?" I said.

"They're picking us up tomorrow night about 7:30. And we're going to ride in a limo with a chauffeur."

"His name is Felix," I said.

"Whatever."

"That's it?" I asked.

"I told you it wasn't a big deal," Heidi said.

"Then why are you acting like this?"

Believe it or not, Heidi blushed a third time. Personally, I couldn't believe it myself, and I was there. "Well," she said. "It's the first time Matthew ever called me."

"Heidi," I said. "you've known Matthew for years. You mean, he never once called you before?"

"I suppose he has," she said, "but this was different. He talked to me."

"Am I just dense?" I asked. "Why am I missing your point?"

"We talked for almost an hour," she said.

"Oh."

"Jennifer." Her words were spilling out now. "It's the very first time any guy has called me and talked a long time. And Matthew's so cool!"

"Right," I said. It wasn't very long ago that I had made the same discovery. And, to be honest, I had felt the very same way. "What did you talk about, or is that too personal?"

"Jennifer," she said. "you're not jealous?"

"Of course not!" I told her. "Why should I be jealous?"

"I was afraid for a minute that you were," she said. "It's really funny, but I'm not sure exactly *what* we talked about. I kept thinking he'd say 'good-bye' but he didn't. He told me about his work at the paint store. And learning to make picture frames. And he wanted to know all about my work for Mrs. Floyd. Just stuff like that."

"And this morning you're still daydreaming!" I smiled at my friend.

"Sounds silly, doesn't it?" Heidi smiled too.

"Not at all," I said. "I know exactly how you feel!"

* * * * * * * *

When I got to my locker, nobody was there. I opened it, hung up my coat, and shuffled my books and homework around.

"Hi, Jennifer." Mack, still in his coat, stood in front of his locker. Which, naturally, is still next to mine.

"Where were you?" I asked.

"What do you mean?" he laughed. "You and Heidi got off first, and took off like a bolt of lightning!"

"Oh," I said. "I didn't realize it."

"Are you really OK?" he asked. "You seem upset."

"Mack," I said, "it's been a heavy morning. I guess I'm not used to doing so much thinking this early in the day."

"Something wrong?" he asked.

"Not really." I wasn't going to mention Walter. Or the moving trucks. And I certainly wasn't going to say anything about Matthew.

"It's OK, Jennifer," Mack said. "You don't have to talk. Can I just walk with you to homeroom?"

I smiled. "Sure," I said. "I'd like that."

We walked slowly, at first not saying anything at all.

"I saw the moving trucks at Baldwins'" I said. "Mack, I felt just like I did when Dad first told us we were moving to Pennsylvania."

"How did you feel?" he asked. "We've never moved."

"Excited and scared all at the same time," I told him. "You know, back then, I didn't realize how good my life here was going to be. It was just one big question mark."

"I remember seeing the van at your house when you moved in," Mack said.

"You do?"

He smiled. "I was hoping there'd be a guy my age in your family!"

I laughed. "What a disappointment I must have been!"

56

"Right!" He laughed too. "When Pete came down to our house with Mike, all I could think of was how unfair life was. We already had Stephanie and Lindsay in the neighborhood!"

I could see Mack's point.

"But the first time I saw you, I knew how wrong I was!"

"That was the day your family took the Green kids to Sunday school," I remembered. "I was so nervous!" I laughed.

"No kidding? I thought you were cool. And, before I knew what was happening, Matthew was calling you for a date."

I remembered the day Matthew called. I had just come in with the mail. And I let the phone ring three times so nobody would think I was too eager. "A lot has happened since then," I said.

"Right." Mack smiled.

And, as we walked into homeroom and silently took our seats, I realized I was feeling better. Lots better.

The bell rang. "I'd like to try an experiment with this class," Mr. Hoppert told us. "I heard about it sometime ago." He paused. "You have a choice whether to do it or not. After I explain the rules, you can think about it, and we'll take a class vote."

We waited. I wasn't born yesterday. I figured the experiment had to be connected with "mainstreaming" the handicapped kids. Maybe I'd have to ride around in a wheelchair. Or act retarded!

I decide to vote *no*. That is, I'd vote *no* if it was a secret ballot. If we just raised our hands and people could see us, I'd vote *yes*.

"The experiment isn't complicated," Mr. Hoppert said. "For two days, the class will be divided into three groups."

I knew it! Maybe I'd be emotionally disturbed!

"Students in Group I can talk to everyone else," he explained. Students in Group II can talk only to others in Group II, nobody else. Students in Group III can't talk to anybody unless the other person speaks first."

Stephanie raised her hand. "What's this supposed to prove?" she asked.

"I think you'll find out that you feel very different about communicating with each other," Mr. Hoppert said. "When the experiment's over, we'll spend some time talking about it. And, maybe we'll write themes."

Naturally, several people groaned. Personally, I like writing, because I'm good at it.

I raised my hand. "How will we know who's in each group?" I asked. "I mean, how can we tell each other apart?"

"Good question," Mr. Hoppert replied. "I'll provide armbands in three different colors."

"Do we have to follow the rules all day?" Scott asked.

"If you decide to try it, the experiment restrictions will apply from the time you leave your home until you return home. So bus stops and bus rides are included."

"How about extra-curricular activities?" Mack asked.

"They'll be included," Mr. Hoppert said. "I don't think two days will goof them up too much."

"How about talking to kids outside of our class?"

Mr. Hoppert thought a moment. "Let's include them too," he said. "If you run into a problem, point to your armband!"

Well, we voted with our eyes open. But actually, it doesn't sound too bad. In fact it could be very interesting.

"What if we can't talk to each other?" Mack asked me, between classes.

"Mack, we'll live," I laughed. "We managed fine before!"

Chapter 8

A Breathless Romance

Lord, it's me, Jennifer.

"You can't imagine what happened last night!" Chris said the minute I walked into the stables.

I took a wild guess. "Jason called you and talked for an hour!" I said.

At first, Chris looked astonished. Then she looked embarrassed. "Oh," she said. "He must have told the Harringtons."

"Wrong!" I said quickly. "You asked me to guess, and it sounds like I just happened to hit it. Right?"

"You mean Jason didn't tell? You're not kidding?"

"Of course not, Chris." I sobered up. "I don't gossip."

"What's the difference between gossip and telling things to your friends?" she asked.

Lord, she's going to be the end of me yet! Frankly, I'm getting kind of tired of figuring things out and thinking and explaining! So, Lord, please help me remember that Chris has nobody else to ask.

"Chris," I said, "you've got to realize that I'm not an expert, but I think gossip is when you're talking about somebody else. And in sharing, you're supposed to tell about yourself."

"I get it," she said. "It's sort of like in Alateen. We're supposed to focus on our own problems, not someone else's."

I had another idea. "Also, I think gossip is mostly telling *bad* things. OK if I clean out the stalls now?"

"Sure," she giggled. "No more questions!"

Maybe she was making up for getting so personal. Anyhow, Chris acted the part of a strict riding instructor during my entire lesson. She even had me mounting and dismounting, the very first thing I learned. Personally, I don't even think about it anymore. But she said I was getting careless about details. She was probably right. Habits aren't necessarily good.

"Whew!" I said afterwards. "That was quite a work-out! Aren't you going to ride?"

"I'm coming back tonight," she said.

"In case you were wondering, Heidi and I decided to wear skirts to the game tomorrow night," I told her.

"Jennifer, I'm so thrilled that Jason likes me! But, I keep thinking I'll wake up and find it's all a dream."

"It sounds to me like you've got a boyfriend!" I said.

"I guess what I've been learning in Alateen is true," Chris said. "The families of alcoholics expect to be disappointed."

"What do you mean?" I looked up.

"We don't even realize it," Chris explained. "But people who live with alcoholics expect that good things will get goofed up. It's like thinking we don't really deserve to be happy."

"I don't know what to tell you, Chris," I said. "Nobody can promise that Jason will like you forever."

"I know."

Then I perked up. "But Jesus will always stick with you!" I told her. "He promises He will. Forever!"

"Are you sure?" she asked. "Can you prove it?"

"It's in the Bible," I said. "I'll look it up. Do you have a Bible?"

"Mrs. Williams gave me one, but I can't figure out most of it. She's going to tutor me so I can catch up."

"Super!" I said. "She's an excellent teacher!"

"Jennifer, I'm so excited about tomorrow night that I can't wait. And Jason *must* like me! I mean, a guy doesn't talk for almost an hour to somebody he doesn't care about, does he?" she asked.

"No, Chris," I said. "I don't think he does." I kept brushing Star and remembering Matthew's call to Heidi.

For a while, nobody said anything. "You say we're wearing skirts?" she asked. "Any special kind?"

"No," I laughed. "Sometimes we wear jeans or slacks. This time Heidi and I just happened to decide on skirts."

62

"I want to do it right," she said.

"Chris," I told her, "any old skirt will do. Relax! Jason *likes you,* remember?"

"Thanks, Jennifer." She was smiling again. "I'm glad you're my friend."

* * * * * * * *

"How are things, Jennifer?" Dad seemed like his old self again! I could sense it the moment I got in the car.

"Basically, OK," I said. "But life certainly can be complicated."

"Growing up isn't easy," Dad agreed. "In fact, even being an adult sometimes has its problems!" He laughed.

Frankly, I was almost afraid to ask. "Are things going better at work?"

"Lots better," he said. A car approached, and I looked at Dad's face in the glare of the headlights. He was smiling his old, confident smile.

* * * * * * * *

Well, Baldwins sure didn't waste much time! When I woke up Saturday morning, a huge moving van was backing into their lane. Their cars were parked, in a row, on our side of the road.

I pulled my shade back down and snuggled under the covers. A person should be able to sleep in one day of the week—without a moving van waking a person up! Right? But, although I closed my eyes, I really couldn't sleep. Once my mind gets up, it doesn't want to go back to bed.

The dumbest thing happened. I kept thinking about Baldwins. Well, to be honest, I kept thinking about Dexter Baldwin-the-Third. The high school guy I'd never met. I rolled over and closed my eyes.

Dexter Baldwin-the-Third came striding into my mind with an air of purpose. His charming smile was deceptive. This was a guy who knew how to get what he wanted! At first, he didn't notice me. And, naturally, I ignored him. I played it cool. I'd let him think I couldn't care less. Which was partly true. His good looks and money might attract some women, but I was different!

Dexter-the-Third climbed into his red sports car and revved up the motor. I could hear it revving. But, naturally, I didn't look up. If I was going to win that spot on the Olympic equestrian team, I had to put riding ahead of everything else. Including romance.

When Dexter-the-Third turned his red sports car into our lane, I wasn't really surprised. I've suspected that, secretly, he has been watching me all year. But this was his first chance to act on his feelings. His father, Dexter Baldwin-the-Second, had been trying desperately to match up his son with the daughter of his wealthy business partner. But now the old man was out of town!

I still never even looked up. I was busy concentrating on the Olympic equestrian team. Of course, Dexter-the-Third didn't realize that. How could he? There was no horse in sight!

He opened the car door. Leaning out, he hoarsely

gasped, "Jennifer!" (He gasped that because Jennifer's my name.) "You don't know how I've longed to gaze into your limpid eyes!"

I still didn't look up.

"Tell me," he said.

"Tell you what?" I asked.

"Am I destined for disappointment? Tell me if you could ever love me!"

I had gotten tired of looking down. So, finally, I let myself look up. He was far more handsome than I had realized! I'd have to watch my step. Keeping out of his trap would take inner strength. Lots of it! "Why, Dexter-the-Third," I said, "I don't even know you!"

"Please call me Dex," he whispered.

"What?" I said. (I said that because I couldn't hear him. Because the car motor was revving too loud.)

"Please call me Dex," he said, louder this time. Now, I could hear him, but just barely.

I decided not to beat around the bush. "What would your father say?" I asked. "And your friends?" I'd feel really stupid saying I could love him and then have him chicken out.

"You're absolutely right," he admitted. "I must think of my father. And my friends. Forget calling me Dex. We'd better stick with Dexter-the-Third."

I felt myself getting angry. "Dexter-the-Third, what makes you think you can ignore me for nearly a year and now expect me to grovel at your feet?" I asked. Breathlessly.

"Don't grovel," he said. Gently, he reached for my hand and helped me to my feet.

Well, I could grovel no more. It is hard to grovel when you're standing up. But now I was afraid. "What do you want?" I asked. Breathlessly.

"I need you," said Dexter-the-Third.

"You're too late," I whispered.

"What?" Dexter-the-Third still couldn't hear me. "I'll turn the motor off!" he said. "Anyhow, all that revving is wasting gas."

Now, I didn't know where to look, so I tried straight ahead. Things were awfully quiet after he turned the motor off. The morning had a thousand ears. I could easily hear his whisper. "Jennifer, I was just telling you that I need you!"

"Oh!" I said. I could think of nothing else to say. "I guess that about says it all," I whispered. Breathlessly.

"Alas!" he groaned. "When I consider all the precious moments we could have had together, my heart is broken! Perhaps, after all, it's not too late!"

"Well!" I said. I could think of nothing else to say. "I guess that about says it all," I whispered. Breathlessly.

"Jennifer!" he said. He closed his eyes.

"Is something wrong, Dexter-the-Third?" I asked. Anxiously.

"It's nothing. It's just that I think I might be going blind." He fought to keep back the tears.

At once, I realized the truth. This guy was no dim bulb. He had me figured out perfectly. I'm a soft touch.

66

Tears get me every time. "Are you sure it's blindness?" I asked. "You didn't just lose a contact lens?"

He missed the sarcasm, totally. "Jennifer, you're brilliant! A contact lens. That must be it!" he said. "And to think I might have never have seen your beautiful face again." He wept, this time, with relief.

"You might not see my face again anyway, Dexter-the-Third," I responded. "Surely you haven't forgotten that you and your family are moving away?"

"No." He couldn't seem to stop weeping. "But I keep hoping it isn't too late."

I looked right at Dexter-the-Third. "Buzz off!" I told him. "You had your chance, Romeo, and you blew it!"

In the end, he had no choice but to face the inevitable. He finally realized that the beauty he had admired from afar, across that very road, had become an opportunity lost. Forever.

Silently, I watched him climb back into the red sports car. Once again, the motor revved. Avoiding my gaze, he put the car in reverse. It was the only way he could back out of our lane. Dexter Baldwin-the-Third turned onto the road. He was a picture of despair.

Once more, I looked down. Perhaps I could still stop him! But was our romance meant to be?

"Jennifer!" Mom was knocking at my door. "Aren't you up yet? You know I need some help this morning!"

It was destiny calling.

Chapter 9

Moving, Out and In

Lord, it's me, Jennifer.

Mom was right. When a person works all week, a person does need a lot of help on Saturday. And Dad had already gone to the office. Personally, I wondered if he would have helped anyway. But I didn't wonder out loud.

"Pete's doing the laundry," Mom said.

"He is?" I couldn't believe it. "I hope he doesn't get my underwear all wrinkled."

"If you complain, you might find yourself doing the laundry next week," Mom told me.

I decided nobody would see it anyhow.

"So," I said, "where's Justin?"

"Who do you think is vacuuming the den?" she asked.

"Aren't you going to ask what *you* can do?"

"I thought I'd start with my room," I said. "And then I'll take it from there."

"Wrong," Mom replied. "I'd like you to work with Justin. Dust the furniture, and make sure he vacuums everything. Afterwards, you can do the bathrooms."

"Right!" I said, trying to keep a pleasant expression.

"I'm heading out for errands and groceries. I suppose every store will be a zoo this morning." She looked tired just thinking about it. But she marched bravely out.

I stuck my bowl in the dishwasher and headed for the den. "Hi, Justin!" I hollered.

It was hard for him to hear me because the vacuum motor was revving so loud. He switched it off. "This is good for the leg muscles," he told me. He turned it back on and continued racing around the room.

"You're suppose to wait long enough so it has a chance to pick up the dirt," I hollered. "Slow down!"

I dusted the tables and the lamps and the desk chair. Frankly, Dad's stuff was all over the desk, so dusting that would have been pointless. In this room, at least, I could keep up with my brother.

After we finished the family room, we took a break. "I had forgotten how big this house is," I told him. "I'll help move those chairs. You might get a hernia."

"What's a hernia?" Justin asked.

Just then, Pete emerged from the basement. "The suds are coming out the top!" he said.

We all ran downstairs. I've heard of billowing suds, but

this was ridiculous! "Did you measure the soap?"

"Of course," Pete said. He slapped his forehead. "Oh, no! I think I measured this load twice!"

"Why is the dryer shaking so hard?" Justin asked. It looked as if it might boogie right out of the room.

"Open the top," I directed.

"You do it," Pete said.

"It isn't my job," I told him. So Justin did it. The dancing dryer stopped entirely. We all peered in. Everything was matted together on one side.

"It's off balance," I said, reaching in to spread the clothes around.

"Want to trade jobs?" Pete asked.

"You're doing fine," I said. "We'll help you scoop out some of the suds." I resisted the temptation to tell him about my underwear.

"The living room doesn't even look dirty," Justin said. "Do you think Mom would know the difference?"

"Of course, she would!" I said. Then I just happened to notice that the big picture window offered the best view of the Baldwins. Well, not really the Baldwins. But we could see the furniture being carried out and loaded into the van.

"I wonder when the new people will be moving in?" Justin asked. "I can't wait to meet my new friend."

Personally, I wasn't that sure. But I hated to admit it. "Maybe you could hang around over there and find out," I said.

"You've got to be kidding," Justin said.

The dining room was a cinch, mainly because we seldom eat there. I could barely tell where my dust cloth had been. "Is this it?" I asked Justin. "Are we done?"

"We have to vacuum Mom and Dad's room," he said. "Then we each have to do our own rooms."

"Want me to help you?" I asked.

"No way," he said. "You just want to see inside my door, don't you?"

I grinned. He grinned back. Our parents' room is at the back of the house, so we could no longer see the movers.

"I still have to do the bathrooms," I told Justin.

"And I have to wash the kitchen floor," he said. "Who do you think has the easiest job?"

"Pete," I said. "He can wait around between loads."

"No, he can't," Justin said. "He has to clean the basement."

"Has Mom been doing this all alone?" I asked.

"Beats me!" He turned on the vacuum.

I was cleaning the powder-room sink when I heard noises. Through the shutters, I could see that a second moving van had arrived. Baldwins must really have a lot of stuff.

Naturally, I needed more light to see what I was doing, so I opened the shutters. That was when I realized that the second van was from a different moving company. The Kings were moving right in! Today! I couldn't believe it.

"Mom, you can't go in there," Justin said. "I just did the kitchen floor."

Mom laughed. "I wish I had a nickel for every time

I've told you that! Did you notice that the new family is ready to move right in as soon as their house is empty?"

Pete came up and joined the rest of us in the living room. Looking out the window was like having the sound turned off on the TV. Only one of the Baldwin cars was still out there. The men were closing the van.

"I need help carrying in the groceries," Mom said. "How's the work coming?"

"I'm on my last load," Pete said.

"I'm on my last bathroom," I said.

"I'll carry," Justin said.

Which is how I missed the final act of the Baldwin departure. See, my parents' bathroom is in the back of the house. I wasn't even watching when Dexter Baldwin-the-Third went out of my life. Forever. For the second time this morning.

"Could I go over?" Justin asked, as we finished our peanut butter and jelly sandwiches. "There's a station wagon parked in front of our house."

"Don't get in the movers' way," Mom said. "And tell the Kings they can use our telephone if they need it."

Justin put on his jacket and left. I was kind of sorry it wasn't like when we were younger. When we all sat on the curb and watched. "Do you think I should go over?"

"It's up to you," Mom said.

I decided to wait. I'd meet Jennifer King soon enough.

Upstairs, while I cleaned my own room, I watched out the front windows. To be honest, I couldn't see anything special. Only that their cars had different license plates.

When I caught a whiff of something baking, I went downstairs. "You're making cookies!" I said.

"Of course," Mom replied. "I've always taken cookies over when anyone has moved into our neighborhood."

"I don't think anybody else does it," I told her. "At least not here." I remembered last summer. "We never saw one neighbor until Mrs. Harrington came down. And nobody brought us cookies."

"*I* do it, Jennifer," Mom said.

"But you haven't even had time to make them for us!" I said.

"It doesn't matter," Mom told me. "We do what's important to us. And, if I'm the last person in the world still baking cookies, I'm planning to take some over to our new neighbors!"

"OK," I said. "You don't have to get so uptight. May I have one?"

I was laying out my clothes for tonight's basketball game when I saw Justin coming back toward our house. With him was a tall, slender guy. Black, of course. They were both smiling.

If I went downstairs now, would it be too obvious? Really, Lord, this whole thing is getting ridiculous! You probably think so too. Right? So I just opened my door and went down.

The guys were in the kitchen. Naturally. That was where the cookies were! I took a breath and went in.

"This is my sister, Jennifer," Justin said. "And, Jennifer, this is my new friend, James King!"

"Hi, James," I said. "Do people ever call you 'Jim'?"

"Nope," he said. "You won't believe this, but my sister's name is Jennifer too!"

"No kidding!" I didn't look at Justin. "Where's Mom?"

"She's taking cookies over to Kings," Justin said.

"They're excellent!" James said. "We never have homemade cookies."

I helped myself to one. There would hardly be enough left for our supper. You're probably thinking "more blessed to give than receive!" Right, Lord?

"Where'd you live before?" I asked.

"Washington, DC," James replied. "Well, really Maryland."

"His dad's with the EPA," Justin said. "That stands for. . . ."

"I know what it stands for," I said.

"I'd better get back, Justin," James said. "They should be unloading my piano pretty soon, and I want to be there. Want to come with me?"

"See you later, Jennifer." My brother grinned over his shoulder. He finally has a friend in the neighborhood.

"Well?" I asked Mom.

"They're lovely," Mom reported, when she got back home. "They had to be out of their house last night. Of course, they're anxious to get the kids in school. And they loved the cookies!"

Naturally, I thought. Who wouldn't? Slowly, I climbed the stairs back up to my room.

Chapter 10

Cinderella McKenna

Lord, it's me, Jennifer.

I had given myself plenty of time. On my bed lay my navy plaid skirt, white shirt, and navy sweater vest. I'd decide about the bow tie later. After my shower.

Ever since I was in Haiti, I've stopped taking water for granted. Naturally, I don't think about it all the time, but the sight and smell of Bat Cave are something you never forget. Every time I take a leisurely shower, I'm thankful for clean, pure, warm, soft water.

I even sang. My voice always sounds better in the shower. It must have something to do with echoes. Right? I hope You enjoyed my rendition of "His Name Is Wonderful"!

At first I didn't even hear the knock on the door. "Jennifer! Can you hear me?"

I couldn't. Which is why I turned off the water. "What's going on?" I asked.

Pete's voice is changing. This time it was high, and I thought it was Mom. He was annoyed. "You have a phone call," he squeaked. Then his voice dropped an octave. "I think it's Chris." It was like having a conversation with several people.

"Tell her I'll call her back," I said.

"You'd better come," he told me. "I think she's crying."

"I'll be right there!" I said. "Talk to her until I come."

As I dried myself off and put on my bathrobe, I tried to figure out what might be happening. I mean, as long as I've known her, I can only remember Chris crying once.

"It's Jennifer," I said, from the extension in my parents' bedroom. I waited.

"I knew things would get ruined!" she sobbed.

"Hey, calm down, Chris. Just tell me what happened." My voice was surprisingly cool and steady. I mean, considering how I felt inside.

"She pulled one of her usual tricks!" Chris said. "Everything was all set for Felix to drive, right?"

"Right!" I said.

"So now she says he can't use the car! It'll get dirty! And she wants it clean for tomorrow's cocktail party."

"You mean your mom?" I asked.

"Who else?" Chris was really upset. "She knew this

was my first real date. And she just wants to spoil it."

I glanced at the clock on the table next to my parents' bed. "Maybe someone else can drive," I suggested. Although it was getting late to change plans.

"Felix told her he'd wash the car in the morning, but even that didn't do any good." Now she sounded mad. "Maybe the rest of you had better just go without me."

I tried to think fast. "What about your dad?" I asked.

"He doesn't know. He thought it was all set. And then he went to an A.A. meeting," Chris told me.

My parents had gone to something connected with Dad's office. I had no idea about Mack and Matthew's parents. Or Heidi's? "Chris," I said, "I'll try to get somebody. Just get ready and quit worrying."

"I am ready," she said. "But I live so far away!" Which was true.

And suddenly I remembered Jason. "Does Jason know?"

"I've been too embarrassed to call him," she said. "He thinks we'll be picking him up in half an hour!"

Oh, boy! Keep calm, Jennifer. There has to be a way! "How about the four-wheel drive?" I asked. "Could Felix take us in that?"

Silence. "I guess so," Chris said. "It wouldn't be as nice, of course. But Mom didn't say we couldn't!"

"Beggers can't be choosers!" I said. Not too original, but it made my point. "What if we keep all the plans exactly the same, only Felix drives the Jeep? Wouldn't that work out?"

"Will we still wear skirts?" she asked.

"That's the least of our worries," I told her. "No changes in plans at this point!"

Chris started to giggle. "Mom will be horrified! No one in our family rides in a Jeep except to the stables."

"A first for the McKennas!" I said. "Hey, I still have to finish getting ready!"

"See you soon," she laughed. "Won't everybody be surprised!"

And here I had been wondering who'd come up to the door for me, Matthew or Mack! That just goes to show that when you don't have anything big to worry about, you can always find something small! Lord, save this night, and make it something special for Chris!

The doorbell rang two times. Which was hardly necessary. The group was only a few minutes late. I had to answer the door myself, which isn't the coolest. But everybody else was either gone or busy. Pete was off again with the drama group and Madeline Claypool. And Justin was across the road at Kings.

"One, two, three, Hi!" Matthew and Mack, laughing like ninnies, were both standing on my doorstep.

I started laughing too. "Looks like a double date!" I said. Which they thought was funny, so they laughed even harder. They each grabbed one of my arms, and we headed out to the car.

"This promises to be some night!" I said.

"No promises!" Mack said. "Just one hilarious evening!"

78

I could already hear laughing from inside the Jeep. Matthew opened the door, and Mack helped me in. I found myself sitting next to Chris. And on her other side was Jason. "Hi, Jennifer!" they both yelled. I mean, they were already wound up!

"On, Felix!" Jason said. "The Stoltzfus residence, please!"

Felix was trying not to laugh, himself. "Yes, Sir," he said. "Do you have the address?"

"Rats!" Jason laughed. "Knew I'd forget something!"

"Turn at the next corner," Matthew said. "I don't remember the number, but I can get you there."

At Heidi's house, the Harringtons went through the same routine. In other words, they left me and both went to her front door. "Be right back!" Mack said.

"Isn't this a blast!" Jason said. "Chris really knows how to put people at ease!"

"You're absolutely right," I agreed. "Hi, Chris!"

"Hi, Jennifer!" she said. Her voice was cheerful and firm.

The brothers returned, with Heidi between them.

"What have we here?" Heidi asked, as they opened the front door of the Jeep.

"The latest thing in chauffeuring," Mack said. "I mean, a basketball game is hardly a formal occasion, right?"

"Right!" laughed Heidi.

It was decision time. The brothers couldn't both sit with both of us. Looking at each other, they kept us waiting while Matthew produced a coin from his right pocket. "Heads or tails?"

"Heads," Mack said. The coin came down. Mack squeezed in beside me. So, naturally, Matthew got in front with Heidi.

On the way to the high school, we were pretty crowded and bumping all over the place. We didn't have a lot of time. But, naturally, Felix didn't have to park. Tipping his hat, he dropped us off right at the door. "See you later, Felix!" Chris said. She was beaming.

We girls waited while the guys checked our coats and got tickets. I glanced at Heidi, and she smiled back. It wasn't long ago that the two of us had come to our first game together with the Harringtons.

"I'm glad you're with us, Chris," Heidi said.

"Me too," she replied. "If I do something wrong, let me know, will you?"

"Chris," I said firmly. "Just remember, you're blue ribbon!"

"Thanks, Jennifer," she said. Again, she seemed to relax.

We had to sit near the top, and the game had already started. Frankly, I hate being late, but I tried not to let it get to me. The guys climbed up the bleachers first, and we followed.

"Chris, you go first," Jason said. Obviously, he had every intention of following her.

"Heidi?" Matthew said. She smiled and slid in. Matthew took my hand and followed Heidi. Which left Mack to bring up the rear. I observed that Matthew was sitting between Heidi and me, and I was sitting between Matthew and Mack. For what it's worth.

I can't speak for Jason and Chris. But the rest of us realized right away that our team was four points behind. And we take winning very seriously. Especially, since Mike Harrington is a star on the team.

We yelled ourselves hoarse, but at the half, our team could do no better than a tie. "If they don't try a full-court press, they've had it," Mack said.

"Really?" I said.

He grinned. "How should I know? Want something to eat?"

"I have worked up an appetite," I admitted.

"You guys hungry?" Mack asked. They passed the word to Chris and Jason, but they weren't. Hungry, that is. Heidi and Matthew decided to join us.

I couldn't believe it. The line for food reached practically around the school. "Is it worth it?" Matthew asked.

We decided it wasn't. Especially since Felix was driving us to Reuben's afterwards. We climbed back up to our seats.

After we sat down again, Mack touched my hand. "I've got a game next week," he said. "Of course, it isn't high school."

"So?" I asked. "Is that an invitation?"

He grinned. "I guess it is."

"Maybe we all could come. Would that be OK?"

"Sure," he said. "But I feel funny suggesting it."

Well, our high school won in a double overtime. By using a full-court press. We all cheered and stood and sang the school song. Chris didn't know the words, but she faked it. I could tell. So what? She was grinning like a ninny.

When we squeezed into a booth at Reuben's, the Harringtons made Jason and Chris sit across from each other. "It's only fair to split you two up for a change," Matthew laughed.

What Chris hadn't realized is that Reuben's after a game is a different place than the rest of the time. You really have to be there. The place jumps. It's loud, and full of jokes and wisecracks and laughter.

Chris grinned at me. Jason thought she was grinning at him. Well, maybe she was. She sure looked happy.

While we ate our hamburgers, I mentioned Mack's game next week. Everybody was enthused about going together again. Mack was pleased. In fact, so was everybody else! Especially Chris.

Afterwards, Matthew and Mack both walked Heidi to her door. Then it was my turn. From my front step, the three of us waved while Felix backed the Jeep out of our lane. Chris and Jason were still inside.

"Hey," I said, "this was lots of fun!"

"Wasn't it!" Mack said. And Matthew agreed. They said they'd see me in the morning and left together.

I stood in the front hall. So, I thought, who needs a shiny limousine, anyway? Like I always say, for a fairy tale, any old pumpkin will do!

Chapter 11

Who Is
My Neighbor?

Lord, It's me, Jennifer.

I should have known You'd hit me with the Good Samaritan today! Like, how obvious can it be!

"Have you met the new neighbors?" Mrs. Harrington asked, as soon as we got into the car.

"I have," Justin said. "At last, I have a friend my own age in the neighborhood. His name is James King."

"A basketball player?" Mr. Harrington asked.

"Nope," Justin replied. "A piano player!"

"I didn't know that," I said.

"He's practically a pro!" my brother announced.

"Jazz?" Matthew asked.

"Nope. Classical."

"You're kidding," Mack said.

"No, I'm not!" Justin said. "He's even been accepted for some classes at Curtis."

I didn't know what that meant. So I just waited. Usually, I've discovered, if you don't know something, somebody else won't know either. And, if you just wait, then he can be the one who asks the stupid question.

"What's Curtis?" Pete asked.

"It's a famous music school in Philadelphia," Mrs. Harrington explained. "You have to be very talented to be accepted there."

"James looks like a basketball player," Pete said.

"So do you," Matthew laughed. "And so do I!"

Then, everybody laughed. Because, although Pete and Matthew are both tall, neither is athletic. As You know. And everybody else does too.

"I wonder if Chris will come to Sunday school today?" Matthew asked, as we walked to our classroom.

"I doubt it," I said. Which turned out to be right.

Well, in Sunday school, we're in the Old Testament. That is my very weakest point. Personally, I think you have to get started on some of those characters when you're a little kid, or it's hard to catch up. I think the heroes all sound alike. Everybody laughs at me. Nobody can understand how I can get Isaiah mixed up with Samson. Do You, Lord?

Actually, it wasn't until the worship service this morning that I really knew You were speaking to me. Clearly! Lord, I do love You with all my heart and soul and mind! At least, I think I do! And my neighbor as myself.

The Good Samaritan happens to be one story I have down pat. We studied it right after I started Sunday school last year, and I got the point. *Everybody in need* is my neighbor! And, yes, it's OK to love myself too. Just as long as I don't become self-centered. I mean, You don't want me to hate myself.

So, I learned, my *neighbor* includes people in other countries. All over the world. You love everybody, and You want me to love them too. This morning, I started thinking that sometimes it is easier to love somebody in another country than it is to love somebody who lives nearby. Like Stephanie. Or Lindsay.

I mean, I never hear far-away people in other countries say bad things. Or act ugly. By the way, do You count war? Or people on television?

I glanced up when the pastor spoke louder. "When was the last time you offered to do something kind for your next-door neighbor?" the pastor asked. "The person in your office? The kid in your class?"

I was caught. There was no getting off this hook. All I could think of was, *Who told him about our neighborhood? Did You?*

And then I got to the real point. Which was why I hadn't gone over to meet Jennifer King.

The funny thing is, Lord, that I don't even know the reason. OK, so I was busy yesterday. And I was thinking about what was going to happen last night. But, the truth is, I'm chicken!

I glanced down the row at Mom. Tired, kind, loving,

busy Mom. Mom, who doesn't know a tenth as much as I do about Christianity. Mom, who spent part of her only day off baking cookies for a family she didn't know. Because being a good neighbor is important to her.

Lord, please forgive me! And help me love other people the way You do!

But, in spite of all my good intentions, this afternoon I stalled as long as I could. I told myself my homework was important. But You know the truth. I was still chicken. It was almost time for youth group before I finally put on my coat. "I'm going over to Kings'," I told Mom.

I rang the doorbell and then stood there. Nothing happened. Just when I was trying to decide whether to go home or try again, the door opened.

"Well, hi!" The man was tall, with a smile that would light up the darkest night. "Have we met?"

I giggled. "I don't think so. I'm Jennifer Green."

"Aha!" He opened the door wider. "Justin's sister! We've been hearing about you! I'm Tom King. Please come in, Jennifer."

I walked into the worst mess I've ever seen in my whole life. It looked like everything the Kings owned was scattered over every inch of the house.

"Sorry about this," Mr. King gestured. "It turned out to be one of my biggest mistakes. I may never live it down!"

I didn't know whether to ask what happened or not. At least, it didn't sound as if they always lived this way. "Is your daughter home?" I asked.

"I should have known," he laughed. "Nobody ever comes to meet me!" He called down the hall. "Jennifer! You have a guest!"

I watched her coming. She is beautiful, with the same smile as her father.

"Jennifer Green is here to see you." He smiled at his daughter. "Justin's sister."

"Hi," she said softly. "I'm Jennifer King. Thanks so much for coming." She seemed poised. And gentle. Kind of like a delicate flower.

"Welcome to Pennsylvania," I smiled. Next to her, I felt like a clod.

"May I take your coat, Jennifer?"

"Thanks, Jennifer." We both laughed. "You're the first Jennifer I've known," I said.

"Really? In Maryland, we had three in our home-room."

"It must have been confusing," I said. "What grade are you in?" I pretended I didn't already know.

"Eighth," she said.

"Same here," I said.

"There's hardly a place to sit down," she apologized. "My room is a bit better. Want to come down?"

"Sure," I said. I walked with her down the hall.

"We've never lived in a ranch house before," she said. "It seems funny not to be going upstairs."

As You probably already know, a ranch house has all the rooms on the same floor. We've never lived in one either. One of my friends in Illinois did, but hers was little. This house is huge. I mean, the end with the bedrooms is as big as my friend's whole house!

She opened the door to her room. I couldn't believe it. "You have wallpaper just like mine!" I said.

"This was Dana Baldwin's room," she told me. "She was our age, wasn't she?" Jennifer asked.

"Dana? We never really knew the Baldwins," I said. "They went to another school." That sounded like I had rejected them or something, so I explained. "Baldwins lived here a long time. We just came last summer."

Both of us perched on the edge of her bed.

"So, you're kind of new too?" she asked.

"Uh huh."

"Are you happy, Jennifer? I mean, has living here worked out OK for you?"

"It took a little while," I admitted. "But now it usually seems like I've lived here forever."

"*That's* encouraging!" She smiled that brilliant smile. And then I watched her look away. "It was hard for me to leave all my friends in Maryland," she told me. "I just couldn't believe it when Dad told us he was transferred."

"I know the feeling," I said. "Jennifer, I can't stay long. I've got church youth group in a little while. I really *have* to go," I told her. "But I was wondering if you'd like me to stop for you in the morning? We can walk together to the bus stop."

She blinked. I couldn't believe it. Her eyes were filling with tears. So I just stared at the familiar wallpaper and kept on talking. "I'll be wearing jeans, myself," I told her. "And probably my pink sweater. Of course, some-times, I wear a skirt, but for tomorrow, I am definitely planning on jeans."

"Thanks, Jennifer."

I glanced at her, and she was smiling again. "It isn't like me to admit this, but, you seem like somebody I can trust. The truth is, Jennifer, I've been kind of afraid."

I didn't let on that I had guessed. Or that I had been afraid too.

We waded back through the cluttered house. "I didn't want to say anything about this mess that might hurt Dad," she explained. "It was supposed to be a surprise. Dad arranged for the movers to unpack everything so Mom wouldn't have to do it. But the guys just emptied all the boxes when we were having supper. Mom nearly had a heart attack when she saw the mess!"

"At least you won't have to unpack a few boxes a day," I laughed.

"Mom doesn't find that very comforting!" she told me.

Frankly, I could see why. I turned the door handle. "I'll stop tomorrow morning about 7:30," I said.

"In jeans!" she replied. "Thanks again, Jennifer!"

Her smile is just like her father's. But now I realize her eyes are different. To be honest, as I crossed the road to my house, I felt like skipping! Remember when I learned to skip? Now, though, skipping isn't considered cool. Anyhow, Lord, I just can't tell you how good I felt! It was even better than fabulous.

Chapter 12

Jennifer's First Morning

Lord, it's me, Jennifer.

I woke up early. In my dream, Stephanie and Lindsay were at the bus stop calling Jennifer King awful names. And I was standing with Mack and Matthew. Looking the other way!

I'm not going to be any good at this, Lord! What You need is somebody with experience. Somebody who is real good at loving everybody. Somebody like Heidi.

The noise I heard had to be Mom. I slipped out of bed, put on my robe, and headed downstairs.

"Hi!" she said. "What a nice surprise!"

"Believe it or not, I've been missing you in the mornings," I told her.

"I believe it," Mom smiled. "I miss you too."

"Is that all you're having? Just juice and toast? After all your lectures on the importance of having a good breakfast? I can't believe it!"

"Don't forget," she said. "I'm the mother."

I laughed. She was right, of course. I decided to change the subject. "How much longer does your computer training last?"

"This particular stage goes through next week."

"What happens to a woman's career when her husband gets transferred?" I wondered.

"It's a problem," Mom said. "A fairly new one. I don't really know the answer."

"For example, did Mrs. King have a job?"

"She certainly did," Mom said. "But moving won't be a problem for her. Maxine King's a model."

"No kidding?" I was impressed. "Have you ever seen her on television or anything? Would I know her?"

"I'm not sure," Mom said. "She told me she's cut back a lot. Now, she does mostly magazine advertisements. She says she's home most of the time."

"Is Maxine King beautiful?"

"*Mrs.* King!" Mom reminded me. "And yes, she is."

"Jennifer's very pretty," I said. "She has beautiful eyes."

"So does her mother!" Mom poured a little coffee into her cup, drank it down, and stuck the cup into the dishwasher. "I have to go," she said. "Hope your day goes well."

"You too," I said. I decided to go ahead and eat.

Back in my room, I nearly forgot to wear jeans! And after making such a big deal out of it yesterday too! My favorites are getting too tight. Then I discovered that the shirt I like best to wear with jeans was in the wash. But I had no choice.

Lord, is this how it is with obedience? I mean, does a person feel like he has a choice or not? In yesterday's lesson, Isaiah just said, "Here am I! Send me!" Didn't he stop to wonder if You might have someone better qualified? Did he feel like he might blow it and wreck everything for You? I suppose You already know my point. Yes, I'm still thinking about Jennifer King. This could be the worst day of her entire life! Does she realize that some people are prejudiced? That kids at school might not even give her a chance?

Well, Lord, I promise to do my best. Not like in my dream. I'll stick right with Jennifer! But You realize I've had my own troubles with Stephanie and Lindsay. Frankly, it's too bad Heidi won't be there from the beginning. She's lived here a long time, and now everybody accepts and respects her. I mean, she was Winter Carnival Queen! Personally, I sometimes have the feeling that as long as I live here, I'll always be new! Were we like this in Illinois?

I tucked my striped shirt into my jeans and fastened the belt. A vest? No, I'd wear a warm jacket. And then another thought hit me! If Jennifer King sits with me, what will happen when Heidi Stoltzfus gets on the bus?

I picked up my stack of books and homework and

headed down the stairs a second time.

"Hi, Jennifer!" Justin stuck his head out his door. But I couldn't see inside his room. It was too dark.

"Hi, Justin," I said. "I'm stopping for Jennifer King."

"Good," he said. "James was worried about her."

As I put on my jacket, I had an idea. I'd sit with Jennifer King until Heidi got on, and then I'd let Heidi have my place. And, Lord, You probably can arrange it so Jennifer will be in Heidi's homeroom. So she will have a friend all day! But on the way down my lane, I started to giggle. I could just hear the Bible verse the way *I* was telling it. Instead of "Here am I. Send me!" it had become, *"Here am I. Send Heidi!"*

Jennifer was waiting for me, with her jacket on. I didn't even have to knock or ring the bell. "Hi, Jennifer!" She smiled her beautiful smile. And, at that moment, I would have done anything in the world for her. Just name it, Lord!

"How're you doing?" I asked. "You look excellent!"

"Thanks," she said. "I'm nervous. But I'll get over it."

"I was like that my first day," I said. We started out.

"Are there other eighth-graders in the neighborhood?"

"Only two girls," I said. "Stephanie Cantrell and Lindsay Porterfield. For boys, there's Mack Harrington. His brother, Matthew, is in ninth grade. Junior high here includes seventh, eighth, and ninth."

"That's how it was in Maryland," she said.

"After a couple of bus stops, you'll meet my friend, Heidi Stoltzfus," I said. "Heidi's in eighth too, but she's in another homeroom." I had talked too much. Jennifer King was starting to look lost. And we were almost at the bus stop. I had no plan. I'd have to wing it. "Help, Lord!"

Naturally, Matthew and Mack came right over. "These are two of the Harrington brothers," I said, "Matthew and Mack. This is our new neighbor, Jennifer King."

"Hi, Jennifer!" Matthew said, smiling.

"Welcome to the neighborhood," said Mack. He smiled too. It was an excellent start! Well, it might have seemed pretty normal to You. But, at my bus stop, I don't take anything for granted. Although Stephanie and Lindsay were standing nearby, they didn't come over to meet Jennifer. It figured. I hoped she wouldn't notice.

"Where are you from, Jennifer?" Matthew asked.

"We moved here from Maryland," she said. Suddenly, she relaxed and smiled. And the sun shone! At least for a minute. Then the bus arrived.

"I usually sit here," I said, waiting for Jennifer to sit down first. That way, I could get up and let Heidi have my seat. If it seemed like the right thing to do.

"Thanks, Jennifer." She smiled at me again. "I think I'm going to make it."

Just then, I heard familiar voices. You guessed it! Sitting right behind us were Stephanie and Lindsay. At first, nothing happened. They were chattering about the party they had gone to Saturday night. I relaxed. But, after the bus turned the corner and everybody was talking, I heard Lindsay's voice. It wasn't really loud. Just loud enough for me to hear. And, naturally, Jennifer King.

"How confusing it's going to be," Lindsay said. "I mean, having two Jennifers in the same neighborhood. Although, I suppose we could call one of them Jenny."

I could feel my face getting red. I wanted to say something to drown out the sound of her voice. But not a word came out.

"Don't be silly," Stephanie laughed. "It will be a cinch. The first one is Jennifer Green. And," she giggled, "the other is Jennifer Black!"

I looked straight ahead, but I wasn't seeing anything. My eyes were filling with tears. I felt angry and sad all mixed together. And I couldn't say a word. Not a single word of comfort. I could feel a tear roll down my cheek. I bit my lower lip.

Why, Lord? Why did you let those stupid girls sit there and say that?

Jennifer King reached over and touched my hand. "It's OK, Jennifer," she said softly.

But she was wrong. It wasn't OK. It was her first day of school in a whole new state. More than anything, she needed to feel accepted. Not different. Not laughed at.

"I'm so sorry," I said. "They're jerks. They've always been jerks. Ever since I moved here."

I was vaguely aware of the bus stopping.

And then Heidi was standing in the aisle next to me. She put one hand on my shoulder. "Hi, Friend," she said. And then she smiled at Jennifer King. "And you must be Jennifer's new neighbor. I'm Heidi Stoltzfus."

"Want to sit here?" I mumbled.

"Don't get up," Heidi said. "I'll just stand next to you, if you don't mind." I could feel Heidi's hand, still on my shoulder. It made me feel alive, connected to reality.

"Hi, Heidi. Jennifer's told me a little about you."

Finally, I was able to open my mouth. "This is Jennifer King," I said. And then I really couldn't believe it. I started to giggle! "You two have something in common," I told them. "Jennifer King, I'd like you to meet Heidi Queen!"

It was pretty dumb, and I'd have died with embarrassment if I had planned to say it. But it turned out to be perfect! It was so off-the-wall that both Heidi and Jennifer started laughing too.

"She does have a way with words," Heidi said. "The truth is, my reign lasted only one night. Yours sounds more permanent!"

"Until I get married, I guess," Jennifer laughed.

"But that's a long way off!" I said. "For now, you're royalty!" Still goofing off, we got off the bus together.

"I'm supposed to go to the office to pick up my schedule," she told us.

"Jennifer," I said, "Remember that you'll have to end up in one of our homerooms. Either mine or Heidi's. And, of course, we'll all eat lunch together!"

"Good luck!" Heidi smiled.

"Thanks." She smiled bravely. Then Jennifer King turned and walked down the hall toward the sign that said "office." All alone. Except for You!

Chapter 13

A Good Neighbor

Lord, it's me, Jennifer.

"She seems very nice," Mack said. He was waiting for me at our lockers. If he keeps this up, the kids will start thinking we're an item. I wonder if Matthew knows?

"Personally," I said, "I don't think Jennifer's any different from anybody else. I mean, everybody feels nervous the first day."

"Then having you introduce her must have helped a lot!" Mack smiled his approval.

I smiled back. "Once I got up the courage to go over yesterday, I discovered the rest wasn't all that hard. You're right. She's really a very nice person."

"Matthew and I were saying, on the bus, that we were

reminded of yesterday's sermon. Jennifer, you're a good neighbor."

"You noticed!" I laughed. "Those verses helped me realize something. A Christian doesn't exactly have the same choices as other people. I mean, a Christian is supposed to act like Jesus would. Right?"

"Right!" he said. "You know, I bet if all of us acted like Jesus, we'd change the whole world!"

"I'm not sure I'm up for taking on the world," I told him. Suddenly, I thought of something I learned about poverty in Haiti. "Well, maybe it's kind of like helping poor people. You change the world one person at a time."

"I haven't thought of it that way," Mack said. "Jennifer, I still think you're a super friend!"

"Thanks a lot," I said.

"You won't forget the game Friday night?"

"Are you kidding?" I said. "It's on the calendar. I'm counting the days!"

"OK. How many?" he laughed.

"Just four more," I said. "Right?" By the time we reached Mr. Hoppert's room, we were smiling like ninnies! I took a deep breath and tired to act cool.

We were in our seats when the bell rang. No Jennifer King. Mr. Hoppert stood up. He said the band is still low on trumpets. Big deal! Some things never change.

Then he said everybody should support our school team at Friday night's basketball game. It's the junior high championship. I hadn't realized the game was so important.

Without thinking, I turned around to smile at Mack. Fortunately, lots of other kids did also.

"We are proud to have one of the players in our home-room," Mr. Hoppert said. Naturally, everybody knew who he was talking about. Mack smiled, but he isn't a show-off. I mean, lots of guys would have acted macho or something. Did Mack act like You would have?

No offense, Lord! I grinned at the thought of You on a basketball team! I'll bet You could even slam dunk! That is, if You wanted to!

Just when I was nearly positive that Jennifer King had been sent to Heidi's homeroom, the door opened, and in she walked. Mr. Hoppert didn't seem surprised. And, to be honest, neither was I. Not deep down.

"Good morning!" Mr. Hoppert said, smiling. I mean, he is one great teacher! And I'm not just talking about English.

"Hi!" Jennifer has one smile, her warm, beautiful one. "I'm sorry I'm late."

"I can guess why," Mr. Hoppert said. "You had to wait in the office."

She nodded.

He must have known she was coming. Mr. Hoppert reached for the paper she handed him. "Class, this is Jennifer King. Jennifer, you may sit in the vacant seat in the fourth row."

Naturally, none of the kids said anything. But we all watched as Jennifer King walked to her place in the va-cant seat in the fourth row. Right in front of Lindsay

Porterfield! I could hardly believe it. Why, Lord? Why?

"Because of our newcomer, I have decided to wait until tomorrow to start 'The Great Experiment,'" Mr. Hoppert announced. "However, you'll find out today which team you'll be on."

The class turned its attention back to Mr. Hoppert. "I'll review the guidelines again," he said. "Group I will be wearing red armbands. If you're a Red, you can talk to everyone else in the class." He held up an armband, which, naturally, was red.

"Group II will be wearing yellow armbands. If you're a member of Group II, you can talk only to other Yellows. Nobody else, though, ever," he explained.

Mr. Hoppert held up a blue armband. "Those students in Group III cannot start any conversation with anyone else. If you're in the Blue group, you must wait until somebody else speaks to you first."

"Jennifer," he said, and I could tell he wasn't looking at me, "we've decided to try a two-day experiment in communication. As I said, we'll begin tomorrow morning. Because you are new, and weren't here when we voted, you can decide if you want to participate. Any questions, class?"

Well, naturally Stephanie had her hand up. It figured. "The only ones who can talk to a Blue are the Reds," she said.

"That's right," said Mr. Hoppert. "Anyone else?"

"Can we choose which group we want to be in?" Lindsay asked.

Mr. Hoppert shook his head. "No. In real life, we can't always choose which group we'll be in."

Mack raised his hand. "Can we tell other kids which group we're in?"

"I'd rather have you keep it secret," Mr. Hoppert said. "Tomorrow, when you start wearing your armbands, the rest of the kids will find out."

Jennifer King raised her hand. "I'd like to be part of the experiment," she said. "I'd like to do whatever all the other kids do."

Our teacher smiled at her. "Fine," he said.

"Group membership will be determined in random fashion, like a lottery," Mr. Hoppert explained. "At first, I considered having you count off around the room—red, yellow, blue, red, yellow, blue," he said. "But I decided against that."

He smiled. "In a minute, you can come up, one row at a time, and select an envelope from the basket. Each one contains an armband for your group assignment. Also, there's a card containing a review of the rules."

"Personally, I'd rather win a million dollars," Bret said. Everybody laughed.

"Sorry," Mr. Hoppert said. "Maybe next month."

We were unusually quiet. I sat and watched the first row go up. Stephanie peeked inside her envelope and made a face. But the others didn't give away what was on their cards.

If I had had a choice, I don't know which group I would have picked. When we walked up, I chose an envelope from underneath. At first, I didn't look inside. But back at my seat, I peeked. My card said, "Group II," and my armband was yellow.

As I reviewed the rules for each group again. I realized I'd be part of a clique. I could only talk to other Yellows. And so far, I had no idea who they even were.

After the bell rang, the kids seemed particularly quiet. In front of me, I heard Stephanie's voice. "This is the dumbest thing I've ever heard of," she was saying.

"Hi, Jennifer," Mack said. He had a funny look on his face.

"Hi, yourself," I replied.

It was the first time Mack's ever walked with me between classes. I was so aware of him and what everybody would think that I didn't pay any attention to the other kids.

"I don't suppose you're going to tell me which color you are?" he asked.

"Are you kidding?" I laughed. Mack might know me pretty well, but not totally. I have always followed the rules. Any rules!

We had just reached our next classroom when I happened to glance around. Guess who was walking with Jennifer King? Lindsay! Yes, Lindsay Porterfield! I mean, I nearly fainted!

At lunch, the girls at our table acted pretty normal. Nobody refused to eat with us or anything. With Heidi there too, I felt like I could handle anything. But nothing happened.

102

After I introduced Jennifer King to the kids who hadn't met her, she was asked the usual questions—where she was from, and how did she like Pennsylvania. That's all people can think of to say to new people.

"Jennifer, are you always so quiet?" Lindsay asked her. That was when I first noticed that Stephanie wasn't at the table. I looked around for her, but I couldn't see her anywhere.

"I don't know." Jennifer King smiled. "My family thinks I talk too much! Especially on the phone!"

The other girls laughed. Everybody could relate to that.

"I'm interested in The Great Experiment," Jennifer said. "Is this something every class tries?"

"Huh uh," Lindsay said. And then she explained it to the kids who aren't in Mr. Hoppert's room. "Some of us may seem different the next couple of days," she laughed. And I mean, Lindsay hardly ever laughs. As You know.

"What's the point of The Great Experiment?" Michelle asked.

"I think it's to show us how differences keep us apart," I said. "And what it feels like."

"Excuse me for changing the subject," Margaret said. "But am I the only one who didn't know our school was in the basketball championship finals? I've never even been to a junior-high game!"

As it turned out, almost nobody had known. But several said they were considering going Friday night. "Want to all go together?" Lindsay asked.

"I'm really sorry," I said. "I already have plans to go to the game."

Heidi said she did too.

"Well, how about the rest of you?" Lindsay asked.

And so that's how Jennifer King got included. Simply because she happened to be sitting at our particular table. Did You plan that too?

After lunch, I walked out with Jennifer. "Want to tell me your color?" she teased.

"Oh, no you don't!" I laughed. "You'll see in the morning!"

Chapter 14

I Get My Turn

Lord, it's me, Jennifer.

I nearly missed the bus for the Twin Pines route. I had left my Great Experiment envelope in my math book, and I had to run back to my locker. In the morning, I'd need my yellow armband.

"Guess what?" Chris said, as I walked in the door.

"If you think I'm going to fall for that again, you're crazy," I told her. "Don't make the same mistake twice," I quoted. "Make a new one!"

She laughed. "Believe it or not, this has nothing at all to do with Jason!"

"I can't believe it," I teased. "I figured it had to be a two-hour phone call this time!"

She got right to her point. "Jennifer, a therapist called the owner of Twin Pines last night," Chris said. "I don't know all the details, but they're going to begin using the stable for a pilot program."

"Astronauts?" I guessed.

"Wrong!" she laughed. "A pilot program means something that hasn't been done before. Remember when we were talking about using horses with handicapped kids?"

I remembered. "They're starting it here? You look excited, that's for sure!"

"They asked me to teach," Chris told me. "Just one eight-year-old girl. And I said I would! The therapist is bringing her over tomorrow after school."

"That's super!" I said. "But I thought we talked about doing it together. Can I help out?"

"Not with her," Chris said. But she was grinning.

"There's more, isn't there?" I asked. There had to be.

"Miss Pagent asked me to recommend someone to work with a twelve-year-old girl. And I suggested you! So she told me to ask if you'll do it. Well?" Chris asked.

I was caught by surprise. "You must think I'm qualified," I said. Chris would never recommend anyone for any other reason. Not if it had to do with horses.

"The therapist will help us," she said. "And those two girls will be the only ones here during that hour. If we need to, we can help each other!"

My excitement was growing. "They're coming tomorrow?"

"If you'll do it," Chris told me.

"Frankly," I said, "I was willing to do it before! Remember?"

"And I wasn't," she admitted. "And you told me it was a way of showing love. And I said I needed all I could get myself." She broke into a big smile! "Believe it or not, all of a sudden I seem to have lots of love left over!"

"I believe it," I laughed. "Which horses will we use?"

"It's up to us. We can use stable horses, but I think Star and Hoagie will probably respond best to us."

I agreed. "For now, let's get those stalls cleaned!" I think I set a speed record for mucking. And then Star and I had our best workout in weeks. Chris even said so.

"What's wrong with the kids?" I asked Chris, afterwards.

"My girl, Shelley, was in an accident. She's partly paralyzed on her left side and can't talk," Chris said.

"And mine?" I asked.

"Physically, she's fine," Chris said. "But she's emotionally disturbed. Her name is Katie."

"Oh, boy!" I said. "I'm glad we'll be together!"

"Me too," Chris replied.

* * * * * * * *

It was good having Dad home for supper. "How's that free-throw streak?" he asked Justin.

"I blew it," Justin reported. "The ball could have gone either way. It rolled around the rim and chose to go out."

"Disappointed?" Pete asked. "You never mentioned it."

"It's not that big a deal," Justin said. "You have to keep things like that in perspective!"

"Why is it that I have the feeling you should be the father?" Dad laughed.

"Horrors!" I said. Justin knew I was kidding.

"How did Jennifer King do on her first day at school?" Mom asked.

"Super," I said. "She's in my homeroom." I looked at Justin. "How about James?"

"Yeah?" Pete wondered. "He was awfully quiet at the bus stop."

"Well, at least he didn't cry!" Justin said. "Like I did!"

"Did James have problems?" Mom asked.

"A couple of jerks gave him grief," Justin said. "It must be hard to be different."

"Because he's black?" Dad asked.

Justin looked amazed. "I don't think so. Because he's into piano playing. They think it's fem."

"That's ridiculous!" Dad said. "Some of the world's most talented musicians are men!"

"Tell it to the fourth grade!" Justin said. "Anyhow, I sure like James. I've always wanted a best friend."

"Do you two have anything in common?" Pete asked. "What do you talk about?"

"That's the dumbest thing I ever heard!" Justin said. "What do you and Madeline Claypool talk about?"

"Madeline Claypool has nothing to do with how James is adjusting in school," Pete said. "And I'm not speaking to you until you apologize. For sure!"

Well, so much for brotherly love. It was great while it lasted!

"Want to hear about toxic waste?" Dad asked.

Everybody groaned.

* * * * * * * *

It's my week on pots and pans. Pete's on loading, and he was irritated that Justin was taking so long to clear. They didn't throw any punches, but my brothers avoided walking upstairs together.

We had had pork chops, and You know what that means! A greasy skillet. Besides, somebody forgot to soak it. Lord, do the little things in life get to other people too?

The telephone rang. I let it ring three times. I didn't want anyone to think I was anxious. However, it turned out to be James. I called Justin, and when I heard him answer on the extension, I hung up.

Lord, so many people are different! In fact, I just realized that *everybody's* different. You must have planned it that way for a reason. Are we supposed to learn how to handle the differences? Are adults as cruel as kids? I was just wondering.

It rang again. The phone, that is. Without thinking, I picked it right up. "Green residence, Jennifer speaking," I said.

"Hi, Jennifer, it's me."

Usually I hate that. I mean when somebody assumes you know who it is. But all I said was, "Hi, Mack!"

"We had a great practice today," he told me. "I think we just might win that game Friday night!"

"How come you never mentioned it's for the championship?" I asked. "I didn't realize it until Mr. Hoppert said so."

"Just humble, I guess," he laughed.

"I think lots of the kids are coming," I said. "It sounded like it at lunch. Will it make you nervous?"

"No. I don't care. Just so you're there!" he said.

I didn't know what to say, so I laughed. "No offense," I said, "but I used to think you were shy."

He laughed too. "That was when I was younger!"

"Hey, guess what?" I said. "Chris and I are going to help two handicapped girls learn to ride horses!"

"No kidding? How will you know what to do?"

"Riding is riding," I guess. "A therapist will be at Twin Pines to help." I told him as much as I knew. "The thing that excites me most is that I think Chris sees this as a way to show love to somebody who needs it."

"How did she think of that?" he asked. When I didn't say anything, he guessed. "Your idea, Jennifer?"

"Well, kind of," I said. "Mostly, it came from Jesus."

"See, you're humble too!" We both laughed again.

I had gone from standing by the phone, to sitting on the floor, and now I was lying down with my feet on a chair. Only a kitchen chair, Lord.

110

It was sort of hard to talk about The Great Experiment without telling each other what colors we were.

"I think we're going to learn more than we expect," I said.

Mack agreed. "I think it's to get us ready for mainstreaming," he said.

"I do too! It figures. Mr. Hoppert came up with the idea right after he read that thing from the principal," I remembered. "Mack, I've been thinking a lot about kids who are different. A few minutes ago, I realized that *everybody's* different—in some ways."

"It's easy to see that in a family," Mack said. "You'd think that four brothers would all be the same. But sometimes I feel as if Mark, Matthew, Mike, and I were all adopted!"

"But you have lots of things in common," I said. "You're all the kind of guys mothers hope their girls will bring home!"

"Is that a compliment?" he laughed. "Why do I feel I've just been called a goody-goody?"

Eventually my father came in and wondered if I intended to talk all night! "Dad wants the phone," I said. "I'll see you tomorrow, Mack."

"Don't forget your armband, Jennifer," he reminded.

"I won't," I said. " 'Bye."

On the way upstairs, I realized that unless Mack's a Yellow, I can't talk to him for two days! And then I realized we had talked for nearly an hour! I grinned. Well, what do You know!

Chapter 15

The Great Experiment

Lord, it's me, Jennifer.

Already last night, I realized it wasn't going to be easy. I mean, I have nothing in my entire closet that looks good with yellow! Forget burgundy! Yuck! I finally settled on my navy plaid skirt, a white shirt, and a navy vest.

After I was dressed, I pinned on the armband and looked in the mirror. It wasn't bad.

Justin surprised me by joining me for breakfast. I wasn't sure if he just woke up early or wanted to avoid Pete.

"So, Justin," I said, "how's it going?"

"I'm happy," he said. He looked it.

"You're very mature about your free-throw streak," I said.

"Thanks."

"I'm glad you and James are friends," I told him.

"Me too."

"So," I said, "and how's it going with that girl you like?"

"What girl?" he asked.

What could I say? The one with the crooked teeth? The one that was so important we had a conference in my room about her? The one that didn't know you were alive, but you liked her anyway? The one whose name you never told me? That one! "I guess it isn't all that important," I said.

"What's with the yellow ribbon?" Justin asked.

"It's The Great Experiment I was telling the family about," I said. "I'm a Yellow, which means I'm in Group II."

"And you can talk to everybody?" he asked.

"No," I said. "That's the Reds. I can only talk to other Yellows."

"And they get to talk to you?"

"Right," I said. This morning it didn't sound like much of an honor.

"Maybe Pete and I should get armbands," he said.

"Do you want to talk to him?" I asked.

"Sure," he said. "But why should I apologize? He was the one who questioned my friendship with James!"

"I hope you work it out," I said as I changed the armband to my jacket. "I've got to go!"

It never entered my mind not to stop for Jennifer King.

113

Again today, she was waiting for me. The first thing I saw was her red armband. She could talk to anybody.

"Hi!" she smiled. "Oh, dear," she said, when she saw my armband. "I've forgotten what that means." She looked on her card.

I wanted to say "hi" so bad, I nearly choked. But the only honorable thing I could do was smile. It reminded me of when I was in Haiti and couldn't speak the people's language. Grandma and I smiled a lot there too.

"Jennifer," she said, "I just want you to know how thankful I am for your coming over to meet me Sunday!"

I smiled.

"And you'll never know what it meant to walk to the bus stop with you yesterday."

I did know. But all I could do was smile.

"I wonder what colors the other kids got?" she said.

Actually, I wondered too. Probably more than she did. After all, I know them better. I shrugged my shoulders.

The first lesson I learned was that being in a clique has certain disadvantages. It cuts you off from everyone else!

Matthew and Mack stood there watching us approach. "Hi, Jennifer and Jennifer," Matthew said. Mack, wearing a blue armband, said nothing.

"Good morning," said Jennifer King. Then she realized that Mack couldn't say anything until someone spoke to him. "Hi, Mack!" she said.

"Hi, Jennifer!" But he wasn't talking to me. He couldn't. Not until I talked to him first. But I couldn't. I just smiled.

"Are you the one who's on the basketball team?" Jennifer asked Mack.

"Right," he said. "Are you coming to the game?"

"I sure am," Jennifer told him.

"How will you manage to practice?" she asked.

Everybody laughed. Even me. Laughing isn't against the rules. Is it?

"I'm not sure," Mack said.

"He'll do fine," Matthew said. "He's always been the quiet one in the family."

"Here comes a Yellow!" Jennifer noticed.

I watched Lindsay walk toward us. She was, indeed, a Yellow. Walking silently beside her was Stephanie, a Blue. Lord, this should prove interesting!

Actually, the only one who could greet them both was Jennifer King. I wondered if she would.

"Hi!" she said, smiling.

"Hello," Stephanie said. I mean, what else could she do?

"Hi, Lindsay!" I said. They were my first words since I left home, and my voice was hoarse.

"Hi, Jennifer!" Lindsay smiled. "Am I glad to see you! Want to sit with me this morning?"

"Sure," I said. "Sounds good."

The bus was coming.

"Want to join me?" Jennifer King asked Stephanie.

"No thanks," Stephanie said. And she turned away.

"Don't pay any attention to her," Matthew said.

"It's OK," Jennifer said. "I'll save a seat for Heidi."

As You know, it's the very same thing I've done all year!

Stephanie took a seat on the left of the bus. At our stop, at least, nobody sat down beside her.

"So," I asked Lindsay, "been riding lately?"

"I've sold my horse," she told me.

"I didn't know that." It was true. She had never mentioned it. I thought she and Stephanie were still riding together.

"You still riding with Chris?" she asked.

"Yes," I said. "Did you know I got my own horse for Christmas?"

"Star, right?" she said. I'm not sure how she knew. Did I tell her? We hadn't talked much.

"Remember that party at Allison's?" she asked.

"Uh huh," I said. As if I could ever forget it! No parents in sight, and guys had crashed the party! And there was beer! Personally, I ended up leaving early because I couldn't handle it. My social life was down the tubes, and I didn't even care!

"You were lucky," Lindsay said.

I nearly fainted. "What do you mean?"

"It really got disgusting." Lindsay made a face. "One guy threw up. And some jerk kept grabbing me until I had to lock myself in the bathroom! I was afraid Mom would never come!"

"I thought I was the only one who was uncomfortable," I said. "To be honest, I figured you'd all think I was a nerd."

"A smart nerd!" Lindsay laughed. Then her face got

116

real sober. "Your leaving early helped me realize how gross the whole thing really was!"

No kidding? Lord, I couldn't believe it.

Heidi had gotten on, and she and Jennifer King were talking away in front of us. I glanced across the aisle. Stephanie was still sitting alone.

At our lockers, Mack and I smiled at each other. Silently. Then we walked side-by-side down to Mr. Hoppert's room. I found out that sometimes you didn't have to talk.

When we opened the door, I nearly fainted. Kids were all out of their seats, and everybody was talking. Well, almost everybody. On the blackboard was written, "THE GREAT EXPERIMENT." *Do your own thing. But quietly, please!*

When the group of Yellows saw me, Scott came over, took my hand, and escorted me to the back left corner of the room. "Hi, Jennifer!" I was greeted by kids who've hardly talked to me before! Lindsay smiled warmly. I smiled back.

It reminded me of camp. It was like we all suddenly had permission to be friends. At least, that's how it was for the Yellows.

In the rest of the room, a few of the Reds were trying to find Blues to talk to. See, Lord, otherwise the Blues couldn't say anything. Some Reds tried to talk to their friends in the Yellow group. But it was no use. Yellows couldn't talk back. Frankly, lots of the Reds just talked to each other. Mr. Hoppert watched. Just before the bell

117

was going to ring, he made an announcement. "You're doing great!" he said. "Just keep it up. If anyone has a special problem, please stop at the desk."

"I have a problem, Mr. Hoppert," I told him. When I explained about what I was planning to do after school, he said it would be OK to talk at the stable.

As the bell rang, all the Yellows decided to eat lunch together. They told me on the way to our next class. Already, we had become a clique.

* * * * * * * *

At Twin Pines, I was pretty nervous. I mean, showing love is one thing, but I have no experience with handicapped people. I don't even know what emotionally disturbed means. Not really.

When I arrived, the girls were already there. They waited on a bench. Chris was talking to an attractive young woman, who had to be the therapist. She has a good haircut and wide hips.

"This is Jennifer Green," Chris said. "Jennifer, I'd like you to meet Miss Pagent. She's the therapist."

"Hi," I said.

She smiled at both of us. "I'm certain you'll do a good job," she said. Then she smiled at the girls. "This is Shelley. And this is Katie."

Shelley smiled a crooked smile. Katie looked exactly like every girl at school, but prettier than most. But she didn't smile. She didn't even look at me.

118

Chris presented each of the girls with a hard hat helmet. "This makes you official riders," she told them. "See, Jennifer and I wear the same kind!"

Our goal for the day was to get them used to the animals.

Personally, my own goal was to get used to Katie. I took her with me while I saddled Star. She watched, but said nothing.

Back in the ring, I stood next to Star and told Katie about horses. "Star's one of my best friends," I told Katie. "And he wants to be your friend too. Come here, and I'll introduce you."

She walked slowly, her eyes on Star. "May I touch him?"

"Sure," I said. I guided her hand. Star didn't move.

"May I sit in the saddle?"

I have a lot of faith in Star. "Well, sure," I said. Talking gently to both of them, I guided Katie through the steps of mounting a horse. And then I asked for Your help.

Although Katie's taller than I am, she seemed small, mounted on the big animal. I looked up at her. "Katie, would you like me to lead Star around the circle?"

Katie nodded. I kept one eye on her all the time. We were nearly around the ring when it happened. Katie smiled!

That might not sound important to some people, Lord. But even Miss Pagent told me it was a big deal. This was the first time Katie had smiled since she came to live at the school!

Chapter 16

Reach Out and Touch Someone

Lord, it's me, Jennifer.

Seeing Katie smile turned out to be an incredible discovery. I didn't realize that helping a person who needed special love would make *me* feel so happy!

Frankly, I think the Good Samaritan should be called the Happy Samaritan! Lord, do other people know this?

Well, the experience with Shelley really affected Chris too. It was obvious.

After the girls left with Miss Pagent, Chris and I started acting hyper! It was the greatest afternoon we've had at Twin Pines in weeks! We were hugging each other and laughing and both talking at the same time. If there's a Cloud Ten, Chris and I were on it!

"How often will Shelley and Katie come?" I asked.

"Just once a week," Chris said. "I really don't think I can wait! Isn't Shelley darling? I'm going to ask the Lord to help both of them! Does He do stuff like that?"

"He's the expert!" I said. I reached into my pocket. "By the way, Chris, I have something for you. It's a promise."

Chris read the Bible verse, Hebrews 13:5, out loud, *God has said, "Never will I leave you; never will I forsake you"*. She smiled at me. "I think it's what I've been needing all my life," she said.

At supper, everybody wanted to know how The Great Experiment was going. Everybody, that is, except Dad. He was in Chicago, meeting with an expert on toxic waste.

"I never really appreciated how neat it is to bc able to talk to people," I said.

"Who can you talk to?" Pete asked.

"Just the other Yellows," I said. "In our neighborhood, the only one is Lindsay Porterfield. We even sat together on the bus!"

"I hear you can't talk to Jennifer King," Justin said. "James says his sister can talk to everybody."

"Right," I said. "Actually, she's very thoughtful. Some of the Reds have missed the point totally. Jennifer realizes that her group is the only one that can help the Blues. Unless a Red speaks to them first, they can't talk at all!"

"Who's in the Blue group? Anybody we've heard of?" Mom asked.

I think I blushed. "Mack Harrington, of course," I said. "And Stephanie Cantrell."

"Do Reds talk to either of them?" Pete asked.

"I don't think I noticed one person talking to Stephanie," I realized. "To be honest, I feel sorry for her. If I were a Red, I'd talk to her."

"James said his sister tried," Justin said. "Maybe it's her own fault. Is it fun being a Yellow?"

"In some ways," I said. "I like the feeling of belonging. But I hate not being able to talk to my other friends."

"Like Mack!" Pete said.

"And others," I told him.

"Sure," he said, smiling.

I decided to change the subject. "How's the computer training, Mom? You're nearly done, right?"

"Right," she said. "But most of the other women have dropped out."

"How come?" Justin wondered. "The reentry isn't working?"

"Believe it or not, it isn't easy to change your life at this point," Mom said.

"Maybe the others don't have your good help at home," Pete grinned.

But Mom was serious. "One woman said she hated to ask her husband and kids for help. She felt that the home was all her responsibility."

I felt kinda guilty. Actually, we haven't been all that swift at offering to help our mother! "How about the rest of the women?" I asked.

Mom thought a minute. "Some women can't handle the risk of failure," she said. "Homemakers aren't used to being judged or graded. And it's been a long time since we've taken a test!"

"Personally, I'm very proud of you," I said.

"Me too!" said Pete.

"Same here!" said Justin.

Mom smiled. "Thanks," she told us.

When we were just getting up from the table, the telephone rang. It was Matthew! "Hi, Jennifer!" he said. "I just thought you might feel like talking to somebody besides a Yellow!"

"Hi, Matthew!" I said. I made a face at Pete who was listening. "I've been wondering. How's your job going?"

"Super!" he said. "How about yours?" He laughed.

"Not funny," I told him. "Somebody has to do it. And my money is changing a girl's world down in Haiti."

"Sorry," he said. "I didn't mean to sound like a clod. Are you still enjoying riding?"

"Matthew," I said. "today the neatest thing happened!" And I told him all about Katie. "I've never felt as happy as when I saw Katie smile!"

"Never?" he asked.

"You know what I mean," I said. "Don't spoil it!"

"I can't seem to get anything right tonight," he said. "Well, anyhow, I was thinking about you."

"Thanks," I said. "Matthew, I really am glad you called." What I said was true. I think.

My second phone call was from Heidi. "Hi, Jennifer,"

she said. "I thought you might want to talk to some-body."

"Thanks, Heidi," I said. "What's new?"

"Not a whole lot. I enjoyed getting to know Jennifer King this morning on the bus," she said.

"Did she eat lunch with you too?" I asked.

"Yes. Where were you?"

"The Yellows all ate together near the windows."

"Anybody I know?" Heidi asked.

"You know everybody in the school!" I laughed. "There's Lindsay, of course. And Scott." I named some others. "It's really strange being in a kind of clique with kids who never talked to me before!"

"Guess what?" Heidi asked. "Mrs. Floyd gave me a raise! And the twins are darling! I just love my job!"

"Tell me all about it," I said.

"I can't now," Heidi said. "When we have more time. OK?"

"I've got a lot to tell you too," I said. "'Bye for now."

My third call was from Chris. I mean, she never calls me unless it's an emergency. My stomach got a knot in it as soon as I heard her voice! "Are you OK?" I asked.

"Never better, Jennifer!" she said.

I relaxed. No crisis this time. "What's up?"

"Nothing. I just wanted to tell somebody how happy I feel. You are the logical person, that's all!"

"I'm happy too," I said.

"That's it!" Chris said. "Hope you don't think I'm stupid or something!"

"Are you kidding? I'll never forget this afternoon!"

"Me neither! 'Bye for now." She hung up. And left me standing there grinning like a ninny.

My fourth call was a real surprise. "Hi, Jennifer!" It was a guy, but I didn't recognize his voice.

"Hi," I said. "Who is this, please?" If it was that jerk from Allison's party, I decided to tell him I'm going steady.

"Sorry," he said. "It's Benjamin Morris. From Mr. Hoppert's class. You know, I'm in the Yellow group. I've been trying all evening to get through to you."

"I have had several calls," I admitted. So? Don't apologize, Jennifer! You don't have to explain anything to him. But somebody had to say something! "How are you doing, Benjamin?"

"I just was wondering if you'd like to go with me to the school basketball game Friday night?" he asked.

I nearly fainted. I mean, until today, he's hardly known I'm alive! For sure. "Thanks for asking me, Benjamin," I said. "But I already have other plans."

"It figures," he said. "But it was worth a try, anyway. See you tomorrow!"

Lord, was it the first time he's called a girl?

The next time the phone rang, it was for Pete. It was a girl. Madeline Claypool? "Pete," I called upstairs, "it's for you!"

I finally finished up in the kitchen and went upstairs. Pete was still talking on the extension in our parents' room. What I mean is, he was holding the telephone to

125

his ear. He hardly said a word. But he smiled a lot. I wonder what Madeline Claypool looks like?

Time goes slower when somebody else is using the phone!

I did all my math homework and went to the bathroom, and Pete was still talking! I realized that nobody else could call me, even if somebody else wanted to.

By the time the telephone rang again, I was in my pajamas and robe. I heard Mom call my name from downstairs.

"This is Jennifer Green," I said, taking over Pete's spot in our parents' bedroom.

"Hi, Jennifer. It's Mack. Mack Harrington," he said.

I smiled. "Hi," I giggled. "You're the only Mack I know!"

"Just checking," he laughed. "Do you think we're breaking the rules of The Great Experiment?"

"I can't remember Mr. Hoppert saying anything about phone calls late at night," I said.

"Good!"

"How did your day go?" I asked.

"I sure found out what it's like for kids who are afraid to speak first," he said. "It's really hard waiting for someone else to make the first move."

"Did anybody talk to you?" I asked.

"Quite a few did," he said. "What's it like being a Yellow?"

"It has its good points," I said. "But I missed talking to you, Mack."

"That's mainly what I wanted to know," he said. Then he was silent.

"Mack," I said. "Are you there?"

"I was just thinking how good it is to hear your voice!" he said. Softly.

I got goose bumps. Even with my bathrobe on!

"Good-night, Jennifer!"

"See you tomorrow," I said. I hung up the phone.

Well, I went to bed. But getting to sleep after that wasn't easy. Eat your heart out, Dexter-the-Third!

Chapter 17

What's on
the Label?

Lord, it's me, Jennifer.

Today, when I got to Jennifer King's house, James answered the door. "My sister will be right down. She forgot her armband," he said. "I see you're a Yellow. What's that mean again?"

"I can only talk to other Yellows," I said. "But today's the last day."

"Has it been hard?" he asked.

I smiled. "Actually, not too bad," I told him.

"Hi, Jennifer! Sorry to keep you waiting," Jennifer said. then she remembered that I couldn't answer, and we both laughed.

I smiled. Just like yesterday.

"You know," she said, "The Great Experiment has turned out to be super for me! I've had a perfect excuse to meet most of the kids in our class! Like a mixer at a party."

I nodded and smiled. I was glad for her. And just when I started thinking the whole thing was a put-up job to make life easier for Jennifer, I realized that Mr. Hoppert had no control of which group she'd be in. Well, scratch that idea!

"I really was dreading school here," she admitted. "It can take forever to prove you're OK."

I remembered feeling the same way. And, of course, I look pretty much like everybody else!

As we got to the bus stop, Lindsay greeted both of us with a smile. But she could only talk to me. "Hi, Jennifer!"

"Where's Stephanie?" Jennifer King asked. But, naturally, Lindsay couldn't answer. "Maybe I'll say 'hi' to Mack," she said, walking over to where he stood.

"So," I asked, "where *is* Stephanie?"

"Beats me!" Lindsay said. "Her mother picked her up yesterday after school, and I haven't seen her since. She didn't even call me last night."

"You didn't call her?" I asked.

"Nope. I'm not sure why," Lindsay said. "I just didn't."

Lindsay and I sat together on the bus again. I wondered if Mack would sit with Jennifer King. He didn't. But I knew Heidi would!

"Mom misses your mother at the neighborhood Bible study," Lindsay said.

"She does?" I asked. "No kidding! Mom's taking special computer training for her job. That's why she's been going every day. But after this week, she'll have Thursday afternoons off again. She likes the Bible study a lot."

"My mom's been thinking of working," Lindsay told me. "But since Dad walked out, she can't seem to get anything together. The Bible study has been Mom's only contact with other women."

"How about the clubs your parents belonged to?" I asked. "Doesn't she have friends there?"

"Nope. Divorce embarrasses them. They don't know what to say to her," she said. "Dad gives us money, but Mom has no self esteem. I'm never going to let that happen to me!"

I wanted to ask Lindsay how she could be so sure. But I didn't. And I wondered if she ever would have told me all this if we weren't both Yellows?

I got to my locker first, so this time I waited for Mack. I pretended to be looking for something. I hope I wasn't too obvious about it. Did You think so?

Mack and I smiled at each other. Then, grinning, we walked silently to Mr. Hoppert's room and opened the door.

I expected it would be just like yesterday. Wrong! I couldn't believe the change! Hardly anybody was talking. Lots of the kids were sitting at their desks. Mr. Hoppert watched.

That's when I glanced at the blackboard. Today it said:

THE GREAT EXPERIMENT

Pick up your labels.

All Reds are unfriendly!
All Yellows are losers!
All Blues are stupid!

I picked up my label from the teacher's desk. Walking back to my desk, I peeled off the back and stuck it on my sweater. *All Yellows are losers!* I was afraid I might giggle. Not cool! Not cool at all. Already, I was starting to feel like a loser! This was really ridiculous.

"What's the matter?" Mr. Hoppert asked the class. "They're just pieces of paper. Right?"

Everybody laughed. Some kids started talking.

"Just a minute," Mr. Hoppert said. "Don't answer out loud! Just think about it. Are the labels true?" He paused. He had our attention, that's for sure.

"Let's start with the Reds," he said. "Are you always friendly? In your heart, you know you aren't! How many Blues did you talk to yesterday? Without one of you speaking first, they couldn't talk, you know! Class, how many Reds spoke to *you* yesterday? They could, you know!"

Some kids started looking uncomfortable.

"Now, let's take the Yellows," Mr. Hoppert said. "You

131

assumed being in your group was an honor, didn't you? But, what if the rest of the class didn't think so? What if they thought you didn't fit in? That you couldn't make other friends?"

He had a good point.

"Yellows, look inside yourselves. Are there times when *you* feel like a loser? Are there good reasons for feeling that way? Reasons nobody else even knows?"

I don't know about the rest of the kids, but sometimes I sure feel out-of-it, Lord! Like in school, when the kids talk about things that happened before I moved here. And even in Sunday school, when I don't know as much as other kids who have been Christians longer. And always when I compare my looks with a really pretty girl!

"And, now for the Blues," Mr. Hoppert said. "Right now you're thinking you have a good excuse for seeming stupid, don't you? But what if you weren't wearing your armband? Do you always know the answers? To everything? Or are you faking it some of the time, just hoping nobody will find you out?"

Everybody was uncomfortable now. "You see," Mr. Hoppert said, "even random, make-believe labels may have some truth in them!"

The bell rang. "Have a good day!" He smiled. But nobody laughed.

Not one Yellow walked with me to our next classroom.

Soon, kids in other homerooms were reading our labels and making sick remarks to us. Or else to each other. But loud enough for us to hear.

"I never realized he was so stupid!" (Laugh!)

"Don't choose her. She's a real loser!" (Laugh!)

"No wonder she has no friends. She's unfriendly!"

"He won't know the answer!" (Laugh!)

As for our class, we really got into The Great Experiment. We became like the labels we wore. And it was awful!

The poor Blues had a day of misery. Of course, they couldn't talk anyway. But the strange thing was that some of them even seemed dumb to me! Not Mack, of course! But I'm prejudiced. And I know he's always been the quiet type.

The Reds, who could have talked to Blues, were so uncomfortable themselves that they didn't bother talking to anyone else. And their *unfriendly* label didn't draw them to each other either.

Suddenly, the Yellows seemed ashamed to be seen together. I mean, who wants to be associated with a bunch of losers!

After school, Chris didn't come to the stables. So I poured my heart out to Star. By six o'clock, even talking with my family at dinner was a downright thrill!

"I never realized just how unfair labeling people is," I said, as I explained what had happened.

"Guess what?" Justin said. "I used to feel stupid!"

"And I was a loser," Pete admitted.

"Personally," I said, "sometime or other, I've felt like all the labels fit. And a few more besides!"

"Me too," Mom said. I nearly fainted.

* * * * * * * *

I got only one phone call, but it was the right one!

"Hi," Mack said. "I hope you don't mind a call from a stupid guy who can't talk until he's spoken to!"

"You called me, didn't you?" I laughed. "And I'm a loser!"

"That just goes to show how stupid I am," he laughed.

I groaned. "Good shot!" I said. "You know, Mack, I may have learned a lot, but I'm really glad The Great Experiment is finally over."

"Me too," Mack said. "I won't even tell you what the guys said at basketball practice!"

"Oh, no!" I said. "You didn't wear your label there?"

"I tried it, just for fun. Talk about dumb!"

"Don't put yourself down!" I said. "Mack, I like you just the way you are!"

"Cut it out, Matthew!" Mack yelled. "My brother wants the phone. I'll see you in the morning. OK?"

* * * * * * * *

Lord, I was never so glad to see a day end! Last night I couldn't decide whether to throw my armband and label in the wastebasket or save them as a reminder.

"Was your day as bad as mine?" I asked Jennifer King.

"Pretty bad! The Reds even stopped talking to each other! Talk about unfriendly!" she laughed.

"Still no Stephanie," I noticed at the bus stop.

134

"She finally called me last night," Lindsay told us. "She's transferring to a private school!"

"Not the one Chris McKenna goes to?" I asked.

"How did you know?" Lindsay wondered. "Do you still want to sit with me on the bus?"

"Well, sure," I said. I wondered if I'd ever get to sit with Heidi again.

"Hey, Lindsay," Jennifer King said. "I'd really like to get to know you better! Could we sit together today?"

"Why not?" Lindsay smiled at us both. "OK, Jennifer?"

It was fine with me. I saved a seat for Heidi.

Well, Lord, The Great Experiment turned out to be such a success that my class talked about what we learned all through homeroom. And later, we continued the discussion all through our English period! To be honest, I was surprised. Mr. Hoppert is usually hard to get off the track. He must have thought that this was really important.

Chapter 18

Championship Game

Lord, it's me, Jennifer.

Word had gotten out. I mean, it seemed like everybody was coming to our basketball game, which was scheduled for the high-school gym. The local newspaper published an interview with our coach. And Mack's name was in the paper! Naturally, I cut it out!

"Why not have Chris over for supper?" Mom suggested last night. "It would make transportation easier. She could ride home with you from the stable."

"Super!" I had told her.

"Could I invite Walter?" Pete asked. "We were planning to go together anyhow."

"How about James?" Justin asked. "I never get to have anybody over for supper."

"Sounds fine," Mom said. "I have lasagna in the freezer."

Well, after supper, we took turns at the phone. When everybody could come, our excitement grew.

Our parents offered to drive my brothers and their friends to the gym. However, Mom and Dad would be permitted to stay for the game only if they promised not to sit anywhere near the boys! Lord, does that sound familiar?

"Hey," Pete said to Justin. "I just realized we're talking to each other!"

Justin grinned. "What do you know?"

"It's funny, but I can't even remember what we were fighting about," Pete said.

"I can't either," Justin said. "But I think it had something to do with James and Madeline Claypool. I'm sorry if I said something wrong."

"Me too!" It was over as quickly as it had started.

As for my friends, once again we'd be riding in Harringtons' station wagon. That is, five of us would. Mack, of course, would be with the team.

This morning, at the bus stop, Lindsay waited for Jennifer King. "I'll clue you in on the plans for tonight," she said.

The Harrington brothers came over to me. "We'll be picking you up early," Matthew said. "We want to get good seats. Right?"

"Right! Chris will already be at my house," I explained.

"Hey, great!" he said. "I'll check to see if Jason can eat with us! Then we'd only have to stop at your house and Heidi's. We should have plenty of time!"

"Hi, Jennifer!" On the bus, Heidi slipped in beside me. It was like old times. "Excited about tonight?"

"Are you kidding?" I laughed. "I could hardly eat breakfast!"

"Did Matthew tell you the plans?" she asked.

I nodded. "To save time, Chris is eating over," I said. "It was just spur of the moment. Pete's invited Walter, and Justin's having James."

"It sounds like an interesting mix of people!" she said.

I had never even thought about that.

Mack was waiting next to our lockers. Smiling.

"Aren't you nervous?" I asked him. "I'm only cheering, and I could hardly eat breakfast!"

"The coach reminded us yesterday that no matter what happens, we've had an awesome season!" he said. "Jennifer, I just hope we do our best and don't disappoint everybody."

I mean, talk about humble! But when I told Mack that, he just laughed at me. We started toward our homeroom.

"You know what?" he said. "Now that we can talk, I can't think of anything to say!" Believe it or not, I couldn't either! Then, just as we got to Mr. Hoppert's room, we both started talking at once. We were still laughing when we got inside.

To be honest, I can't report that The Great Experiment has totally changed our homeroom. But, personally, I think kids seem friendlier. And even happier. Lord, do you agree?

* * * * * * * *

Before supper, Chris and I were getting dressed in my room. "Are you sure I look OK?" Chris asked. "I'm so excited, I think I need another shower!"

"You look excellent," I said. "Do you like these earrings?"

"The little balls look better!" she told me.

I took the hoops out. I probably shouldn't have asked. Chris is the frankest person I've ever met.

When Mom called, we were both ready.

It turned out to be one of the most fun dinners we've ever had! Everybody was in a good mood. Any concern I had about people feeling uncomfortable was gone before we even prayed.

"This lasagna is excellent!" Walter knows delicious when he tastes it! "With your busy schedule, how did you have time?"

Mom beamed. "I had it in the freezer for a special occasion. And tonight I'm celebrating the end of my computer training!"

Everybody cheered. Including Chris and James and Walter.

"I'm proud of you, Dear!" Dad said. "Does anyone else have reason to celebrate? How about you, Jennifer?"

"I survived The Great Experiment!" I said.

"Let's hear it for Jennifer!" So everybody cheered again. We were really getting into it now. And it was fun!

"Justin, anything to celebrate?" Dad asked.

"I apologized to Pete, and we're talking to each other again," he said, smiling. We all cheered, especially Pete!

"Chris?" Dad asked.

"I have another date with Jason!" She was smiling from ear to ear. More cheers! And a whistle!

"How about you, James?"

"I made it through the week!" he reported. Because we all know how that feels, we cheered particularly loud for him.

"How about you, Pete?"

"I have a new friend!" He smiled at Walter. And we all cheered. Including Walter!

"Your turn, Walter."

At first he seemed unprepared. "I feel like I belong!" Walter said. He grinned, almost like a ninny. I mean, we have ninny down pat! But Walter came close! When the rest of us finished cheering, he said, "How about you, Mr. Green?"

Everybody looked at Dad. "I love my family!" he said. "Everyone here included!" The place went up for grabs!

No kidding, supper was fantastic, Lord! Even though we ran low on lasagna. To be honest, I don't think anybody except me noticed. Well, probably Mom. And maybe Walter.

Later, by the time the doorbell rang, Chris was a nervous wreck. But once she saw Jason's smile, she was OK.

140

She didn't notice another thing. For sure. And neither did he!

Matthew had come to our door with Jason. Smiling, he offered me his arm. "May I?" he asked.

"Sure." I smiled and linked my arm through his. We followed Chris and Jason to the car.

"Jennifer, I promised Mack I'd take good care of you," Matthew told me. "So he can concentrate on the game!"

"Thanks, Matthew," I said. A few minutes later, I watched him, tall and confident, as he walked up to Heidi's door.

"Hi, everybody!" Heidi said. And the station wagon was filled with happy voices. Except for Mr. Harrington. He was invisible and silent. But that didn't keep him from smiling! He'd be staying for the game. For sure!

We found excellent seats—right in the middle, eight rows up. Matthew arranged it so I sat between Jason and him, with Heidi on his other side.

We talked as we watched the gym filling with people.

"I was supposed to work tonight," Matthew told Heidi and me. "Fortunately, I was able to trade off with another guy."

"Hi!" I yelled. But Jennifer King didn't hear me. She was coming in with Lindsay and the lunch-table kids. I never did see my brothers. To be honest, I didn't look too hard.

"I'm glad Jennifer King could come," Heidi smiled.

To my right sat Jason and Chris. Jason wasn't exactly

rude. He just never realized I was there! I grinned over at Chris. She saw me and smiled back.

Loud cheering announced that our team was coming on the floor. And, from that time on, I was conscious of only one person. You guessed it, Lord! Mack Harrington.

Soon, the crowd had joined me. Each time Mack got the ball, everyone yelled. At the half, we were ahead by fifteen points. And Mack had made fourteen of them!

"He's even better than his brother!" said a man in back of us. I wondered how Mack would feel being compared to his oldest brother. And then I remembered Matthew, sitting next to me. I noticed him as he started talking to Heidi.

"It's a great game, right?" I said to them.

"Awesome, Jennifer!" Matthew said. He smiled at me.

"'Marvelous Mack'!" Heidi named him.

"I'll have to remember that one!" Matthew laughed. "'Marvelous Mack' Harrington!" Then, in a totally natural, almost unconscious move, Matthew took Heidi's hand and smiled at her. And she smiled back. I've never seen Heidi look so happy.

Personally, I looked back down at the empty gym floor. There was nowhere else to look.

"Just think what this Harrington kid'll be doing in three more years!" said the man behind us. "And I hear there's another brother coming up!"

However, the opponents weren't dummies. When the game started again, they double-teamed Mack. It worked. Our other players missed shot after shot. Even

142

Dunk Boswell couldn't buy a basket. Frustrated, Mack quickly collected three fouls. Frankly, I thought one was a bad call, but what do I know?

The crowd watched in disbelief as our lead dwindled away. Even the cheerleaders couldn't spark any genuine enthusiasm!

Well, in the movies, the hero always gets inspired by spotting his girl friend in the stands. But, as You know, Mack never looked up. I don't know if it really would have helped or not.

Now the score tipped back and forth. And the yelling started up again. "Mack! Mack! Mack! Mack!"

Mack finally got the ball and broke away from his guards. He ran almost the length of the floor and, at nearly the last second, he passed the ball to Dunk Boswell.

Well, we won! The crowd went crazy. Everybody screamed and hugged each other. Even Jason hugged me, if You can believe that! Chris watched and laughed.

"I told you, didn't I! Keep your eye on Harrington!" said the man in back, in a loud voice.

The team carried the coach out of the gym on their shoulders, just like on TV. That's probably where they got the idea.

"I'm starved!" Jason said, finally. The rest of us had waited what seemed like forever for Mack to dress and join us. At last, the team came out of the locker room.

Grinning from ear to ear, Mack headed our way. I honestly was wondering if he'd hold my hand in

Reuben's. That's how dumb I was. What really happened was more incredible!

While we all watched, Matthew left Heidi and the rest of us, and ran toward his brother. The two guys grabbed each other and stood there together, talking and laughing. Then, both smiling, and with arms around each other's shoulders, Matthew and Mack walked slowly back to where the rest of us waited.

Only then did Mack smile at me. I have to admit, it *was* a goose bump kind of smile! Dropping his arm from Matthew's shoulders, Mack looked right at me. "Your turn, Jennifer!" he said. And, while the other kids cheered, Mack hugged *me*!